SHORT STORIES

INCLUDING A SHORT STORY WITH SHORT ALIENS

JAMES BOHUN

Erstun Press

Copyright © 2024 James Bohun

All rights reserved. No part of this book may be reproduced in any form or by any electronic or mechanical means, including information storage and retrieval systems, without written permission from the author, except for the use of brief quotations in a book review.

ISBN 979-8-9897653-0-0 (print)
ISBN 979-8-9897653-1-7 (eBook)

CONTENTS

PREFACE	v
1. A SHORT STORY WITH SHORT ALIENS	1
Part I: The White House—The First Two Years	*3*
Part II: The White House—Years Three and Four	*19*
Part III: The White House—Running for a Second Term	*25*
Part IV: The White House—Years Seven and Eight	*35*
Part V: The Post-Presidency	*41*
2. LO'S GALACTIC ADVENTURES	49
Part I: Lo's Name	*51*
Part II: Lo's Friends	*59*
Part III: Mommy's Wrath	*65*
Part IV: The 3GA Galaxy	*69*
Part V: The Primterrean Secret	*73*
Part VI: The Erstun Galaxy	*75*
Part VII: The Earlies	*83*
SCIENCE FICTION GLOSSARY	89
ABOUT THE AUTHOR	93

PREFACE

These short stories are arranged in chronological order, opening in the twenty-first century with "A Short Story with Short Aliens." The short stories close in the distant future with "Lo's Galactic Adventures."

This book is classified as science fiction because it deals with extraterrestrial beings. It is actually historical in nature, based on events that will happen in the near future, soon to be the past ("futorical"). Obviously, the names of the innocent—and guilty—have been changed.

You may find the "Science Fiction Glossary," located in the book's end, helpful when reading the relevant short stories.

A SHORT STORY WITH SHORT ALIENS

A SHORT STORY WITH SHORT ALIENS

PART I: THE WHITE HOUSE— THE FIRST TWO YEARS

Harold Carson successfully ran on a third-party ticket in the United States 2036 presidential election. Both major political parties disgusted voters after decades of hostile bickering.

President Carson, born at the turn of the century in the midwestern United States, was the youngest person ever elected to the presidency, surpassing even President John Fitzgerald Kennedy, who was a youthful forty-three years of age when elected. Many people believed that President Carson was almost as handsome as President Kennedy.

Carson, a green-eyed widower with brown hair, had spent nearly twelve years laboring for global peace. His most notable action was providing a solution to Middle Eastern hostilities.

President Carson's first year in office was a dismal failure since Congress did not pass any program he advocated. Usually, members of the House passed bills the president favored. This was a political ploy to gain constituent support when up for reelection. The House members would put responsibility for nonpassage on the Senate. After all, it was in the Senate that all of Carson's supported bills died, killed by his adversaries.

Senator Lawrence (Larry) Slick of the Republican Party and Senator Robert Wiley of the Democratic Party headed the opposition parties. These former rivals joined forces because of the loss of their candidates during the election. They were determined to bring Carson's administration down, with hopes of their favored candidate winning the 2040 election.

Carson's senatorial foes took great pleasure in annoying him on a personal level as well. Instead of referring to him as Harold, his appropriate given name, they called him "Harry," a nickname the president detested. The only other insult that infuriated the president more was when his political rivals sang or played "I'm Just Wild about Harry."

Early in the second year of President Carson's term, he visited Dayton, Ohio, campaigning for yet another favored program. He was summoned to the nearby Wright-Patterson Air Force Base and provided with information about the government's contact with alien entities from other worlds. Many of his questions went unanswered because nobody had the answers, but the response to his query about why he was being told of this now was that the most advanced civilization, the Primterreans, had requested to meet with him.

President Carson was ushered to the base's massive underground complex to an area where a communication center with interstellar capabilities was located. After he was left alone in a "contact room," an alien appeared on one of the walls that had a silver screen. The most pronounced feature observed by the president was the large head housing a brain undoubtedly much larger than that of any human and, obviously, with far superior intelligence. The body was long and slender, with lengthy, twiglike arms and legs lacking any noticeable muscle. The Primterrean reminded Carson of an old-fashioned wooden clothespin but with arms that extended down to about its knees. He could tell the being was tall, but it was difficult to estimate its height without an in-person appearance.

President Carson started the conversation. "My name is Harold Carson, and I am the president of the United States, the leader of this section of our planet."

"I am Sponsor, and I am your contact with my civilization, the equivalent of an ambassador to your society. I will answer any questions that a representative from your world is entitled to at your stage of development. I will not answer questions we deem you are not allowed at this time. We use the same methodology for all worlds we contact to assist in their advancement."

The president had been assured that the contact room was totally private and no one would be aware of their conversations. He was also told that although their conference would last for hours, only seconds would pass outside the contact room; hence, he could tell inquirers only what he wanted during the subsequent debriefing.

Carson learned much from Sponsor, and he was pleased the experience also educated the alien as to his belief that the knowledge of other beings should be shared with the rest of the world. Sponsor agreed and, in fact, told the president of a future event. In a few weeks, there would be an unusually warm winter day on which a White House press conference would be held on the lawn. A member of the press would ask Carson if he believed in life on other planets. That would be the indication that a craft would appear and the first public contact with extraterrestrials would take place.

A fortnight later, Sponsor's prediction became reality. Initial questioning from journalists on the White House lawn dealt with Carson's continued policy failures. Upon calling on another reporter, the question was asked: "Mr. President, do you believe in life on other planets?"

The president said, "With the hundreds of billions of stars in our galaxy alone, each containing a number of planets, the likelihood of other life is highly probable; in fact, I believe there is life both more and less intelligent than humans."

A hand jetted upward from one of Carson's contentious press affiliates. He called on the antagonist, who asked, "Aren't you afraid that your political opponents will point to that statement and say you are mentally unfit to continue to serve as president under the Twenty-Fifth Amendment and seek your removal from office?"

"No!"

"And why not, Mr. President?"

"If you'll turn to your left, my answer is self-evident."

To the gasps and awes of the press, an alien craft silently and gently landed on the opposite side of the White House lawn, apparently having evaded radar. Within seconds, a ramp was lowered, and three aliens appeared, clothed in uniforms remarkably similar to those worn by airline pilots.

President Carson walked to the craft, followed by the press corps engaged in photographing this historic event. Some members of the media were in disbelief—others were in shock—at what they were seeing. When Carson was within several feet of the craft, one of the extraterrestrials stepped forward, with arm extended, and shook the president's hand while saying in a female voice with an American accent, "My name is Independence, Mr. President. I have taken that name because all say I am fiercely independent."

A second extraterrestrial stepped forward with hand extended and spoke in a female voice with a British accent. "My name is Victoria, Mr. President. I have taken that name due to my studies of your civilizations and the attraction I had for the British."

The third extraterrestrial, speaking in a female voice with an Australian accent, said, "My name is Matilda, and, like Independence and Victoria, I set my translator to the language and accent of my preference."

"My name is Harold Carson," said the president to the chuckles of the press.

The only similarity between Sponsor and the three representatives he noticed was their large hairless heads, but the three had larger eyes and a grayish tint to their skin. Additional facial features included a petite nose with nostrils that were more prominent, a lipless mouth, and recessed ears. Below the head was a long neck attached to a tree-trunk-like body without a waistline. Their short, slim legs supported the body, and long, skinny arms extended from the shoulders to the pelvis. At between four and four and a half feet, they were considerably shorter than adult humans. These beings were Altwainians, but people referred to them as Twainians or Twains.

Altwainians have a genetic disposition not to harm any sentient being.

Additionally, under Primterrean direction, Twains use their robust desire to assist less advanced civilizations through the development of superior technology. Primterreans and Altwainians had improved the lifestyles of hundreds of societies across the galaxy, and it was now the people of Earth who would benefit.

The Altwainians offered rides to press members so that they could experience weightlessness above Earth after the artificial gravity field was turned off. Their craft was capable of holding forty people per trip, so the entire press corps had an off-planet experience within hours. The press conference ended as sunset approached. The extraterrestrials were offered a stay in the White House private residence as the president's guests.

The following morning, President Carson woke to see the three Twains at the foot of his bed, with six oversize eyes staring at him. He asked, "How long have you been standing there, and is everything all right?"

Independence said, "About an hour of your time. We usually rest about three hours, and as we grow older, longer, until we sleep between eight and nine hours and death sets in. We worried about you since you slept so long."

"It's normal for me and other people to sleep between seven and eight hours every night."

"We apologize. We also were wondering about something strange we saw on the thing on the wall. There were children with pink circles coming from their mouths that kept getting bigger until they broke."

"It sounds like you were watching television, and the children were probably blowing bubbles with gum. I can have my staff give you some bubble gum, and someone will explain how to blow bubbles. Also, there's a press conference scheduled for noon, and I'd like the three of you to attend; you'll sit in the front row. As you can imagine, there will be a multitude of questions about you and other life in our galaxy."

Based on the information given to him by Sponsor, President Carson was fielding answers to questions quite well. He noticed Independence remove a package of bubble gum from her pocket and offer it to Victoria, sitting immediately to her left. The president thought to himself, *No, don't take any.* She didn't. Sitting to Victoria's left was Matilda. Independence offered her gum, and she took two. The president thought, *No, please don't chew.* Too late—Matilda put both pieces in her mouth and chewed. Then the unthinkable happened. Matilda blew a bubble that grew and grew until Independence reached across Victoria and poked Matilda's bubble, breaking it. Matilda sat with bubble gum on her face as camera flash after flash lit the conference room, with Matilda's pink and gray face as the target. Carson knew it could not be good and dreaded reading what would follow in the newspapers.

That evening, the president's nightmare transitioned to reality when the headline in a rag read, "Galactic Bore." The publication summed up the headlines in many newspapers and electronic media, and so did its story, emphasizing that extraterrestrials had to travel hundreds of light-years just to be bored by Carson.

The old cliché "adding insult to injury" did not apply to the next incident from the legislative branch. Instead, it compounded the injury exponentially. Due to the alien influence in the White House and the jeopardy it posed to national security, Carson's administration was required to have a mandatory security specialist, under the auspices of the Senate, overseeing it; the severe backlash from Senators Slick and Wiley was unanticipated. They had coerced Carson to agree to the supervision under the threat of impeachment and removal from office. Senator Wiley said, "We have the votes in both the House and Senate." Carson knew they did.

President Carson realized that there was a tremendous financial economy funded by the secretive alien technology program hidden from society. Not only did this program self-fund experimentation and development, but this "good old boys' network" also provided a lavish lifestyle for those involved. His administration's economists estimated that the loss to the clandestine program over the next century would not be in the paltry millions or billions, not even in the pittance trillions, but several quadrillion dollars. Fear of losing their monetary benefits caused them to retaliate. Furthermore, Carson had exposed the nearly century-old cover-up scheme of disinformation orchestrated by the conspirators, with the resulting loss of their credibility. Those conspirators now shifted their focus and used fear and prejudice to gain allies, indicating that the world would lose its identity and be assimilated into an alien culture.

The early-morning hours brought Senators Slick and Wiley to the White House with an introduction to Mr. Jonathan Jones, the Senate's private security specialist.

Mr. Jones essentially had the extraterrestrials confined to the White House residence, without access to their craft, which was hauled away to a military base. Fortunately, the aliens had activated a field that would prohibit entrance to the craft. At least two of the Twains were needed to deactivate their security net. Mr. Jones also planned to limit their exposure to the public through mandatory "introduction to Earth" classes, consuming their daytime hours. More draconian measures would follow. The president gave the extraterrestrials the option to leave the White House; they chose to stay and continue their assignment. In the interim, Carson told the Altwainians to use the West Sitting Hall, outside his bedroom, as a workplace.

Zelda Needles, a seasoned veteran in television media interviews, worked for a broadcasting company whose management was openly unfriendly to President Carson and his administration. They managed to arrange a one-hour interview in a White House setting with the president, who had hopes that extraterrestrial exposure in homes would win favorable public opinion. Mr. Jones had a heavy influence on the selection of the broadcasting company.

As fate would have it, the day of the interview was dreary and rain-soaked. After consulting with the company's psychologists, Zelda's producer insisted she wear a bright-orange dress to create a distraction and undermine the president.

The first question Zelda asked was about the aliens. It was anticipated, and President Carson's response was rehearsed well. He asked Zelda to write a word on a piece of paper and show him the word; she wrote "sunglasses." The president then called Independence into the room. After introducing Independence to Zelda and, of course, the viewers, Carson stated that the Altwainians could communicate using psychic means through touch. He demonstrated by touching Independence, who left the room and returned with a pair of dark sunglasses, which Carson put on and wore for the remainder of the meeting. Upon completion of the interview, Jones's security personnel escorted Zelda out of the room. As she approached the exit to the White House residence, all three Altwainians bid her farewell wearing dark sunglasses.

The change of seasons in 2038 also brought global changes—the most notable of which was a general international acceptance of the extraterrestrials, with several nations saying they would welcome a number of Twains as immigrants. That was heaven-sent news for President Carson because Sponsor and, more recently, Independence had indicated that the inhabitants of Cimmaclay were interested in sending Altwainians to Earth. This planet was a world with beings more similar to humans than the other extraterrestrials.

Residents of Cimmaclay, known as Clayites or Clays, had bald heads just noticeably larger than those of humans. Their average height was only inches less than Earth's people, and their remaining features were remarkably similar. Extraterrestrials had made contact with Cimmaclay only about two centuries earlier, and thus their society was not too much more technologically advanced than that of Earth. The greatest exception was their interstellar travel and interaction with numerous other species. Primterreans, Altwainians, and Clayites were the three main extraterrestrial civilizations that humans would have contact with for the remainder of the twenty-first century.

In the spring, a fourth member was added to President Carson's household. Her name was Kitti, and she was a youthful stray gray tabby cat that Independence adopted. The president had evidenced a little quirk in his personality since childhood—he always kept a clean pair of pajamas under his pillow for use in the evening. Kitti discovered and took advantage of this peculiarity. Carson found that Kitti had the annoying habit of jumping on his bed, putting her paw under his pillow, and removing the fresh pair of pajamas the president had placed there. Kitti would then carry the pajamas, in her mouth, to any spot where she wanted to take a daytime catnap. She especially loved his flannel pajamas.

Kitti provided Independence with the company most Altwainians enjoyed because they had what they called "twins." Of course, all Twains looked alike, and the majority of humans could not tell the difference between them; however, the reason Altwainians used the term *twin* was because of similar thought patterns. The mental connection between two Twains bonded them to one another for much of their life span, which averaged 250 years on our planet.

Another significant change in the White House was that some of the news media mocked Carson by stating he was the Altwainians' daddy. When Victoria learned this, she asked if it was all right if they referred to the president as "Daddy." She explained that Altwainians are not born like humans but, rather, birthed. Through the birthing process, Primterreans create or birth Altwainians in what humans would consider a hospital laboratory setting. As such, they have no father, and most Twains lose contact with the Primterrean who births them, considered their mother, once they leave the Primterrean home planet (Primterrea), located relatively close to the center of the Milky Way galaxy. After years of education on Primterrea, Twains are transported to other worlds, with the goal of advancing civilizations by aiding in the improvement of the engineering, mathematical, scientific, and technological development of the indigenous population. In effect, as explained by Victoria, Twains are the galaxy's orphans. The president agreed to the "Daddy" connotation, and it proved to be a turning point. With the responsibility of Altwainian "children," he would soon go on the offensive to protect both his girls and his administration.

A few evenings later after a typical vegetarian dinner, the "family" relaxed in the White House living room. Kitti was snuggled up to Independence when the president said, "My pajama top was outside Kitti's litter, being used as a doormat, and she needs to stop this bad behavior. I'm going to have an animal behavior specialist train her."

"Why?" questioned Independence. "I'll just ask her not to do that."

As Independence rubbed Kitti's head, the cat replied with several meows.

"She promised no more pajamas near the litter. Kitti also said that she'll do anything I ask because I'm very pretty and you're not."

"Do you really expect me to believe that?" He added in jest, "After all, most people consider me handsome."

Victoria and Matilda chimed in, indicating they could also communicate with animals.

Stunned by the information provided, Carson questioned, "Can you both receive information from and transmit information to all animals, particularly dogs?"

"Yes."

"Can dogs understand what humans say?"

"Some words, such as commands, but usually not. However, anything dogs overhear is stored in their brains, and we can find it and decipher it in our minds. Dogs are very smart, you know."

"Meow!"

"Yes, Kitti, you're absolutely correct. Dogs are *almost* as smart as cats."

An audible purring came from Independence's lap.

"Would you be willing to help Daddy get information from some dogs?"

"Of course, Daddy," was their collective response.

President Carson planned to go for broke. He wanted every congressional bill he had favored for the past eighteen months that did not pass to be rolled up into one enormous bill. In all likelihood, the House would pass it, as was their routine, and the Senate would not—just as they had in the past. Therefore, he knew he had to concentrate on senatorial votes.

The president enlisted the girls' aid in planning a number of small gatherings at the White House over the course of the next months. The gatherings' completion left sufficient time for a vote weeks prior to the November midterm elections. In each session, the guests were limited to a few senators, their families, and most important, their pets—nearly every senator had a dog. Carson barbecued and simultaneously lobbied his program while the girls gave baths to the dogs. Subsequent to each gathering, there was a debriefing session in which the girls relayed information needed for "shrewd political manipulation"—the term Carson used for what others deemed blackmail.

With the knowledge that the most difficult senators to convince to vote for his agenda were Slick and Wiley, President Carson invited them to the Oval Office. After providing them with his awareness of their misconduct, he assured them nothing was to be made public if they voted for his program.

Slick said to Wiley, "I told you never to use a credit card; Harry was able to track down everything you did."

"Yeah, but you use cash all the time, and he still found out about all your—putting it mildly—'activities.' How was that possible?"

The three politicians realized Wiley raised a highly valid point.

Slick said, "Tell us how you found out."

"No."

"If you don't tell us, we won't vote for your bill, right, Bob?"

"Right, Larry!"

Carson was not going to give up his girls; however, a thought flashed in his mind that could turn this into a win-win situation for the girls and him. He made his response more convincing through a show of reluctance.

"I'm not giving up my source."

"Then we're outta here. Let's go, Bob."

"Wait a minute. Are you really willing to risk the ruin of your careers over finding my source?"

"Yes" and "yeah" were their responses.

"Well, I guess the most important issue here is what the American people want and need. So if I give you my source, then you'll vote in favor of the bill and also won't interfere with other senators voting for it; is my understanding correct?"

"There are some good points in your program that will benefit my constituents, so that's a positive for me," said Slick.

"Me too," said Wiley.

Matilda had been very methodical in her retrieval of information from Slick's and Wiley's dogs when she gave them baths. She had told her father who Slick's "banker" was.

"It's Mr. Jones," said the president.

"I told you there was something about Jones that I didn't like," said Wiley. "I never want to see that rat again or have anything to do with him. Ship him off to our moon base."

"What moon base?" asked Carson.

"We have a top-secret moon base, which is on a need-to-know-only basis," said Slick.

"Well, he needed to know since we're transferring Jones to the executive branch—make sure he doesn't step foot on this planet again for a very, very long time. I'll send you his personnel file later today," said Wiley.

As anticipated, the House of Representatives passed Carson's favored comprehensive bill, and he worked on "convincing" other senators of the bill's benefits; it squeezed through the Senate, and the president signed it into law.

With Mr. Jones commencing his lunar sojourn, the process of dismantling his distasteful security bureaucracy in the White House residence began; Jones was now security chief of the moon base, with Victoria as his Oval Office contact. Of primary importance was reducing Jones's mandatory Altwainian two-year introductory course to Earth, created to keep the Altwainians from interacting with humans. Twains were well educated on Primterrea prior to departing that world; the sciences, mathematics, and arts were far more advanced than on Earth. In fact, the girls had educated themselves on Cimmaclay about much of the customs and history of Earth and particularly the English-speaking nations.

Now that the girls had the run of the White House, rather than being restricted to the second floor, they interacted frequently with its staff. Additionally, Independence started a social media account on life in the White House, drawing millions of followers.

Nigel was assigned to the private quarters and, as a consequence, came in contact with the extraterrestrials more than other people. His father was an overseas diplomat for the State Department and was instrumental in getting Nigel a position in the White House.

Victoria and Matilda spent time in the third-floor workout room. At least once a week, the entire family went downstairs to the bowling alley. Because bowling was a new game to the girls, they initially threw many gutter balls. Matilda, the most athletic of the three, had a rapid improvement in her score from the midseventies to the midhundreds, challenging the president, who averaged about 170 per game.

With the year's end in sight, the president explained the significance of Thanksgiving and Christmas to his "daughters." For Christmas, Kitti's "grandpa" gave her a gray flannel blanket, with hopes of it relieving his "missing" pajamas situation. It helped somewhat, but on occasion, he would find his pajamas on the couch, wrapped around a napping cat.

It was during the holiday season that the family sat down and planned the acquisition of Altwainians from Cimmaclay. Independence explained that most crafts built for the Clayites involved a certain group of Twain laborers, who had aged over the past two hundred Earth years. This was the main group of Altwainians the Clayites sought to send to Earth because they were nearing life's end; some needed costly, extensive care. Independence and her sisters were sexagenarian youngsters in comparison. The Clays also wanted to deport advocates for the elder Twains, like the girls. If Slick and Wiley had knowledge of the Clayite plan, they would have opposed it, probably saying something to the effect that the Clays were dumping their burdens on Earth.

On the contrary, according to Independence, elders would instruct and train humans on the construction of interplanetary crafts, eventually turning over this highly skilled technique to Earth's people.

President Carson recognized Independence's great organizational skills from the aid she provided during the senatorial sessions. She also had superior negotiation abilities, which proved fruitful during discussions with Cimmaclay on the plan for accommodating millions of Altwainians on Earth; the negotiations moved forward. One important point was that payment to Earth would be through providing countermagnetium, the element necessary for interplanetary travel. The Twains would be responsible for its safe storage.

Interstellar travel involved more sophisticated science and technology and a large "mother" ship. Earth would not receive this knowledge for another century.

A SHORT STORY WITH SHORT ALIENS

PART II: THE WHITE HOUSE— YEARS THREE AND FOUR

More than a year later, a treaty between worlds was completed and ratified. Additional good news resulted from the midterm elections, with President Carson's party making gains. In the interim, the girls enjoyed their earthly home, and their favorite leisure activity was clothing shopping using their father's credit. Independence once used it to have a temporary tattoo that said "Daddy" put on her pinkie. The White House staff had an inside joke that she had the president wrapped around her little finger.

One White House staff member noticed something unusual about President Carson. While giving Carson a haircut, the barber spotted a gray hair growing out of the president's scalp. A discussion brought forth the fact that most presidents tended to develop gray hairs while in office—after all, Carson was pushing forty.

The girls rejoiced at their father's news and looked forward to his full head of gray hair because gray was their preferred color. Kitti's meow made the vote unanimous. Additionally, Matilda quipped that no Altwainian ever grew a gray hair, which received a laugh from the president since he knew they were entirely hairless.

Related to gray hairs, of course, was the aging process. The Twains always provided age information in terms of the time of the planet they inhabited. Victoria explained that one year is the time it takes a planet to orbit its star, whereas a day is the time it takes a planet to turn once upon its axis in relation to its star. Cimmaclay had shorter years than Earth, as well as shorter months and days. Victoria further stated that during interstellar travel, they would not age, in accordance with Albert Einstein's special theory of relativity; aging would occur only when on terrestrial bodies such as Earth or Cimmaclay. That aging is referred to as *planetary individual maturity* (PIM). Additionally, Einstein believed that large masses such as stars influence space-time by bending it. Simply put, swift interstellar travel is accomplished by finding and using the bend in space-time between the current location and the one being traveled to. In effect, this is a shortcut, or a wormhole, reducing travel time to a fractional proportion of what it would otherwise take.

On Cimmaclay, Altwainians worked twice the number of hours of Clayites and had no benefits; they were overworked and repeatedly complained to the Primterreans. As a consequence, Independence was sent there and organized other Twains on Cimmaclay to advocate for the aged. The result was that Altwainians received some benefits, with a work scale that reduced the number of hours worked depending on age. Clayites realized the negative impact on productivity but had little choice when the Primterreans intervened with a threat to withhold technology, which was of far greater importance than reduced productivity.

To help combat future abuses of working Altwainians, Independence had established a committee of Altwainian shepherds to oversee the interests of her people prior to departing Cimmaclay for Earth; her dedicated lieutenants, Victoria and Matilda, had assisted her. The committee was composed of the most skilled engineers, technicians, and scientists necessary for the development of further Clayite space flight and technology; not ceding to additional Altwainian demands would stagnate the Clayite advancement.

The Altwainians on Cimmaclay knew that the Clayites' extreme avarice had gained them the moniker "Avarytes" among other alien civilizations.

Part of the treaty between worlds was that the Altwainians would receive two craft-manufacturing centers on Cimmaclay; this had an astute rationale behind it. There were five types of interplanetary vessels, numbered craft one through five; craft-one, the oldest and smallest, held ten people. Earth had developed the small vessels using alien technology in their clandestine program exposed by President Carson. Each craft in the numbered sequence doubled the number of occupants, with a maximum capacity of 160 people in craft-five. As the size of the crafts grew, so did the technology needed to construct and operate the more advanced vessels. Earth was now allowed to have the craft-two technology and the machinery to build them, overseen by the Altwainians.

The Altwainian reasoning behind constructing older craft-two vessels on Cimmaclay was to use craft-five technology in them, saving an enormous amount of valuable material, especially countermagnetium, in constructing the craft-two vessels. The Twains had the knowledge to accomplish the conversion. In fact, Altwainians were regarded by most extraterrestrial civilizations as master craftspersons of vessel construction, and their skills were held in high esteem. Twains either completely constructed crafts on other planets or, under their guidance, oversaw the construction by the indigenous people. Under the Altwainians, the safest and highest-quality crafts were built.

Altwainians knew they would profit immensely by leasing these updated interplanetary vessels to wealthy Clayite sightseers. Affluent Clayite citizens did indeed seize the opportunity to privately tour their solar system's most desired locations and often added the premium option of Altwainian pilots and tour guides. Independence had learned the importance of a monetary system on Cimmaclay and the power that wealth commands. And the Altwainians found unforeseen allies to support their venture in the Cimmaclay solar system—the inhabitants of the outer planets and moons profiting from the elite-tourist expenditures. Moreover, the Twains received support from the construction industry needed to build new structures and the tour agencies vying to have the Altwainians service their clients.

Altwainians arriving on Earth had used their construction skills to update the craft-three vessel initially given to the girls by the Clayites. They tested it, and Matilda independently confirmed all revisions functioned properly. The girls wanted to demonstrate the craft's new abilities to their father and invited him on a trip "once around the planet."

In space, the functionalities were shown to the president and his Secret Service agents. One update left the greatest impression on all the humans. It involved viewing outside the spacecraft.

Matilda explained that craft-one vessels had the ability to change a small section of the craft's walls into portholes to view space. She showed them that feature and continued to demonstrate the other viewing options. Craft-two vessels involved seeing through all walls; craft-three added views through the ceiling; craft-four through the floor, to the gasps of the earthlings—several were afraid they would fall out into space. Craft-five viewing astonished everyone, and the president's comments summed up the others' opinions.

As Matilda implemented the final viewing option, the president said, "What happened to my legs? They disappeared." He felt them with his hands and added, "Oh, they are still there. I can feel them. Wait a minute—my hands and arms are gone, too! This is a truly amazing option, a one hundred percent view of Earth and space with nothing to obstruct the view, not even ourselves. And I can even see the sun without squinting my eyes. Truly amazing!"

Independence said, "There's one more extremely important functionality added. We can communicate with the Primterreans directly without having to use one of the contact rooms on Earth. This ability was actually borrowed from mother-ship technology that has that capacity."

The president thought that was convenient since he would not have to travel to other areas, such as Camp David, to contact the Primterreans and asked, "Aren't you afraid my security will leak that information?"

"Look at them," said Independence.

Her father turned and saw the agents motionless; he knew that they were outside the craft's contact area and, thus, frozen in time.

Just then, Sponsor appeared and said, "Greetings, all."

"Greetings, Sponsor," said the president.

"Greetings, Mother," said Independence.

"Mother?"

"Yes, I had spoken to her when our engineers first installed the contact technology on this craft. We agreed it was time you knew that Sponsor birthed me and the reason. Mother will explain."

"Due to the unjust treatment of our children on Cimmaclay, our elders' council decided a special individual was needed who would not be subservient but, rather, independent in her own thoughts and actions to advance Altwainian work conditions. Based on all the Altwainian children I had birthed over the ages, I was entrusted to birth—or in this case, sponsor—such an individual; she stands beside you."

"And you did a spectacular job, Sponsor. Do I understand you correctly that your name is derived as a result of sponsoring Independence? I was under the impression that you were named Sponsor because you were Earth's benefactor when it came to our introduction to other civilizations."

"In regard to contact with your planet, I took the name Sponsor with a dual purpose: the primary reason was my child, and your understanding is the secondary purpose. Do you have other questions?"

"It seems to me the Altwainians have greater telepathic abilities than is generally known, and they can communicate without touch. I base this statement on my observations of their interactions with one another when no one is around other than me. What is their true telepathic ability?"

In the blink of an eye, President Carson suspected he had been frozen in time and asked, "What just happened?"

Sponsor said, "I spoke with the Altwainians after I delved deep into your mind and determined you could be trusted. They agreed to share with you that Altwainians are the second-most-advanced telepaths in the galaxy. Due to past interactions with other civilizations, their superior mental capabilities caused suspicion among some people, leading to hostilities against the Altwainians. They are a peaceful species, unable to defend themselves except by avoiding or running from violence. The Altwainians, therefore, imposed a strict tenet not to use their broad telepathic skills—only those involving touch. Additionally, they value other species' privacy and only use their full psychic powers when interacting with other advanced telepaths or when in life-threatening situations. Primterreans respect the Altwainian wishes and have long kept their secret." Sponsor turned to the girls and said, "Before I leave, I want to remind you to tell President Carson what you did while we spoke and he was in suspended time. Farewell."

"What did you do?" asked the president.

Independence produced a picture with Carson holding a sign saying "Altwainians Rock" with the girls dancing beside him. The president thought it cute.

Unknown to the president, Independence later posted the photo on her social media account. His advisers called it to his attention and stated it was their belief the picture would cost him millions of votes in the upcoming election campaign.

A roar came from the Oval Office, "*Independence*!"

A SHORT STORY WITH SHORT ALIENS

PART III: THE WHITE HOUSE— RUNNING FOR A SECOND TERM

Quite on the contrary to what the advisers expected, Independence's photo gained President Carson a multitude of votes from strong supporters, who purchased items such as T-shirts and coffee mugs with the picture on it. Now it was not only a favorite symbol in the United States but had also received international acclaim. Carson's re-election committee grabbed the opportunity to make the image the centerpiece of his campaign.

One of America's most beloved social media celebrities, Kitti, got in on supporting "Grandpa" by posing for an "Altwainians Rock" photo with "Mommy," Aunts Victoria and Matilda, and the president dancing beside her. Daily posts of Kitti in the White House by Independence had made her the world's most famous cat. Kitti now always wore a "Reelect Carson" button in her day-to-day posts.

Reelection was a struggle, but with the power of the incumbency and his team, President Carson achieved victory over the two major-party candidates and, once again, took the oath of office on January 20, 2041.

One morning weeks later when the president came to breakfast, he immediately noticed the girls were dressed in new outfits and complimented them. They thanked him for his approval and the use of his electronic debit card to purchase the clothing. He was especially impressed with their guest's ensemble: a flamingo-pink blouse with lilac pants and a snow-white cummerbund.

President Carson said, "Independence asked me if you could stay the night. I approved and notified the Secret Service. She also said your name is Taylor."

Taylor rose from her chair, stepped toward him with arm extended, and said in a French accent, "That's correct, sir."

As they shook hands, Victoria said, "Taylor started garment manufacturing, and our apparel was acquired from her line of clothing—it is all made in the United States."

Matilda said, "And Taylor made the T-shirts that helped you win reelection."

"It would be really great, Daddy, if Taylor could stay permanently so that we can help her plan the extension of her business. Profits would be used to help aged Twains," said Independence. She played the nepotism card: "It would make Mother extremely happy."

"Well, one thing I never want to do is to make Sponsor unhappy since I don't want a rain cloud eternally parked over the White House. Yes, you can stay, Taylor. I'll notify the staff."

"Oh, Mother would never do that."

"It was a joke, Independence."

"I get it, Daddy. And it was a very good one. I believe with all the difficulties you receive from Congress, there is a metaphorical dark cloud always hanging over the Capitol Building. But on a serious note, can Taylor's twin, Penelope, stay permanently as well?"

"Taylor's twin, Penelope! Of course Taylor has a twin. More than ninety percent of Altwainians have twins," said their father.

Victoria said, "Penelope designed the aircraft uniforms we were wearing when you first met us. You really liked them. Please, Daddy."

Matilda added, "They can share the same bedroom like Victoria and me. Pretty please, Daddy."

"I'll notify the staff that we will have two more residents."

In addition to fashion designing, Taylor and Penelope had an inclination for music; Taylor played the piano, and Penelope played the violin. They made daily use of the music room in the White House. After each session, Taylor enjoyed a slice of coconut cream pie in celebration of her skill at the keyboard. Nigel always ensured that the White House had a fresh supply of coconut cream pie on hand.

As winter's snow waned and the nation's capital enjoyed the annual arrival of its cherry blossoms, the new girls experienced success in their garment expansion. They had settled in their new home and called the president "Daddy." They also celebrated mastery of their preferred musical instruments. President Carson liked Taylor and Penelope's playing so much, he scheduled a recital for them with congressional members present.

On the day of the performance, Senators Slick and Wiley approached the twin musicians and made a secretive request that they play a certain song as a finale to surprise their father. Both senators held a grudge for their parties' candidates losing a second time to Carson. Noticing the two men talking to the twins in the distance, the president took a few steps and put his arm around Matilda, causing her to look up at him and smile. He communicated to her, requesting she use her psychic ability to ask Penelope what his opponents wanted. Matilda relayed the response to the president. Still touching her so that he could talk to her privately, he said, "Tell your sisters this is what we are going to do."

Taylor and Penelope received standing ovations with the completion of each piece played. Penelope, speaking in an Italian accent, announced that the last work was at the request of members of the Senate. Just then, President Carson, Independence, Victoria, and Matilda walked on the stage and sang along as the

Altwainian musicians played "I'm Just Wild about Harry"; most of the audience joined in.

Summertime marked the arrival of the remaining shipment of parts for Earth's first interplanetary vessel manufacturing center. The United States had already completed construction of the complex to house it, and assembly started. The initial shipment of countermagnetium from Cimmaclay was soon to arrive. The eastern European nation of Midlandyya had won the international lottery to receive the second production center; most of its parts had already arrived.

In a congratulatory teleconference call, the prime minister of Midlandyya insisted President Carson call her Svetlana. He reciprocated by stating she call him Harold. Arrangements were made for her to come to America to finalize the agreement with a signatory conference. Ordinarily, a nonstop jet flight from Midlandyya to the United States would take about nine hours. Svetlana completed her trip in less than one hour since she experienced space flight—the Twains used their craft to transport her to Washington. At the flight's beginning, Svetlana complimented the girls on the aircraft uniforms they wore, which Penelope had designed. Additionally, during the flight, while Matilda piloted the vessel, Svetlana "talked" with Victoria through touch telepathic communication. Their conversation centered on the president, with the prime minister asking what his likes and dislikes were; Svetlana reiterated the parts she was interested in, and her entourage took notes.

Svetlana's embassy staff had already delivered flowers to the White House, and the president told her he appreciated it very much. He recalled that the only person to ever give him flowers was his late wife. Svetlana stated that she and her late husband had a similar custom of exchanging flowers—fresh-cut tulips from Holland—just like the Carsons. Each one talked about the loss of their spouse in turn and the grieving they experienced. Even after the conclusion of the formal ceremony for the second craft production center, the chiefs of state continued their personal conversation. After sunset, the president invited Svetlana to stay at the White House. Customarily, visiting international leaders would stay across the street at Blair House. Once the press got wind of Svetlana's overnight visit, headlines read "Carson's Blue-Eyed, Blonde-Haired Bombshell." As their relationship expanded, so did Svetlana's stay in Washington; they had extraordinarily similar interests, no doubt due to Victoria's influence. Alas, all good things end, and the prime minister returned home.

Svetlana's departure did not end their relationship, however, as it blossomed during the remainder of the year. Svetlana returned to the United States and received a presidential guided tour of the construction of the first craft-two interplanetary vessel being produced on Earth. In turn, Harold visited Midlandyya to explore the construction of their manufacturing center for interplanetary vessels; completion would be in time for the arrival of the last shipment of parts for Midlandyya's industrial complex by year's end. The 2042 new year began with Svetlana and Harold announcing their engagement.

Taylor and Penelope's first-anniversary date of entering into the Carson family arrived. For dessert, Taylor enjoyed a second piece of coconut cream pie. The president said, "Taylor, it appears your daily snack of coconut cream pie has caught up with you—you've put on weight during the past year."

The four other Twains behind Taylor nodded in agreement with their daddy.

Taylor said, "No, Daddy. My clothes have shrunk."

The others shook their heads, indicating Taylor's statement was inaccurate.

Once more, the president said, "I believe you have gained a significant amount of weight during the past twelve months."

Again, the four other Twains nodded in agreement.

Taylor reiterated that her clothes shrank and turned to her sisters, asking, "Isn't that right?"

They nodded in agreement, causing the president to think, *What a bunch of wimps!*

Their father said, "We'll have an impartial party make a decision. Tomorrow, we'll go to the doctor's office."

The following morning, Taylor weighed in at fifty-one pounds, substantially below the Twain normal weight of between sixty and sixty-five pounds.

President Carson said to Taylor, "Take off your shoes and drop them to the ceiling."

"You mean the floor, Mr. President," said the doctor.

"No, Doctor, watch this. Taylor, do as I instructed."

With the first shoe off her foot, the doctor was mesmerized as it floated upward, followed by the second shoe.

The president asked, "Where are your sisters?"

"In the workout room."

"Let's go."

Upon entrance, Carson was greeted with an Altwainian facing him—upside down!

"Get off the ceiling, Independence."

Looking to his left, Carson commanded, "Victoria and Matilda, get off the wall."

Then Penelope said, "What about me?"

The president glanced to his right and saw Penelope doing a slow horizontal rotation about three feet above the floor.

"And that goes for you, too. Get off the . . ." He hesitated. "Air? You know what I mean—Penelope, walk on the floor! You know countermagnetium is extremely precious, and if you're going to be cavalier with the first shipment from Cimmaclay, how can you possibly be trusted in the future?"

"But, Daddy . . ."

"No, Independence. Don't interrupt me. I know it takes four of you to release the security ring around the countermagnetium, and you are undoubtedly the ringleader. This countermagnetium is the property of the United States, and as president, I have the responsibility to ensure no one misuses it. I also know that this is an infringement of common sense."

Victoria interrupted her father. "That's untrue, Daddy. I suggested we help Taylor with the countermagnetium to reduce her weight on the scale. Independence is the only one who had nothing to do with releasing the security ring to obtain a few specks of countermagnetium."

"Then I proposed we take a little bit more to test the quality of the countermagnetium, just to confirm it was up to enriched standards, since the Clayites cannot be trusted. It appears this batch of countermagnetium meets specifications," said Matilda.

"I'm astonished at the two of you. In the future, I want you to oversee our scientists during their testing of the countermagnetium. And I apologize to you, Independence."

"Is that because I'm the good one?"

The bubble-gum incident flashed through the president's mind, along with all the criticism he had to endure as a result of that unfortunate event. On the other hand, Carson knew that Independence was good-hearted and behaved in a beneficial manner to those she dealt with. The president said, "Yes, you're the good one, Independence."

"Hear that, everyone—I'm the good one."

Midlandyya's prime minister decided to take a different approach to vessel building than the United States. Svetlana felt that having Altwainians train humans on vessel construction in conjunction with building them impeded and slowed the process. Since the Americans had a six-month head start over Midlandyya, she proposed to have strictly Altwainian craftspeople construct their initial vessels, with hands-on training to come later. The result of Svetlana's prudent logic was seen just prior to the midterm elections, when Midlandyya had completed two vessels, which were tested/approved by the Altwainians, whereas the Americans were in the midst of the testing phase of their first vessel.

Midlandyya auctioned both crafts with the expectation of receiving bids in the tens of billions of dollars. Final bids far exceeded their expectations—both crafts surpassed the $100 billion mark from two rival mining companies, one American and the other from the European Union. Each company sought to stake a claim to resources on other planets/moons ahead of competitors; they would recoup their investment multiple-fold.

During the November 2042 elections, President Carson and his allies made gains in Congress, including Senator Wiley being voted out of office, ending his decades-long tenure.

With the approaching holiday season, the Carson family presented White House staff members with a present they longed for, a trip into space. It also offered the president and his girls the opportunity to contact Sponsor on Primterrea. Once they linked the craft's communication to her, Carson said, "Something has puzzled me since our last discussion aboard the Altwainian craft. Weren't my Secret Service agents suspicious they may have been suspended in time like I was? And they may have overheard our discussions, just like my staff now."

"I will not allow them to remember anything."

It was implicit in Sponsor's statement that she allowed Carson to remember.

Independence said, "I asked Mother to let you recall because I'm the good one."

Sponsor gleefully said, "Yes, child, you're the good one."

From the doting manner in which Sponsor spoke to Independence, the president knew Independence had informed her mother of the words he said to her during the countermagnetium incident involving Taylor's weight.

He looked at Victoria and Matilda and added, "All my girls are good. Thank you all for the trust you put in me."

Days later, President Carson was in the White House residence with Nigel when the girls returned from a Christmas shopping spree and thanked the president for the use of his credit. He expected the usual parade of newly purchased garments. Instead, to his astonishment, they surrounded him and held their right hands out, and each had the word *Daddy* tattooed on their pinkie. Independence said, "Don't worry. They're all temporary."

After President Carson thanked the girls and they left, he said to Nigel, "That's true. They have me wrapped around their little finger, but I fear it is not temporary."

The president then sat on a couch to relax when Kitti jumped up, walked across his lap, jumped down, walked across the room, and made use of the litter. The president said, "Look at that, Nigel—even the cat walks all over me."

A SHORT STORY WITH SHORT ALIENS

PART IV: THE WHITE HOUSE— YEARS SEVEN AND EIGHT

January 2043 brought the announcement of a June White House marriage—the first wedding of a president inside the residence in more than a century.

The children were ecstatic about the upcoming wedding and volunteered to help in its planning. Svetlana said she would be happy to have their input and added it would provide the opportunity to listen to both Taylor's and Penelope's accents as they applied their professional apparel skills to her wedding; she loved the way they talked and gave them hugs of gratitude. In reaction, the joyful twins did "ballerina" spins. Six Twain eyes stared intently at the president—Independence spoke what Victoria and Matilda also thought. "Daddy, you never give us hugs."

"Come here, girls," said their father as he hugged each one.

Independence did what resembled an old-fashioned square dance while Victoria, Matilda, Taylor, and Penelope did ballerina spins. This incident proved that four out of five happy Altwainians do a ballerina spin.

Shortly thereafter, on a Saturday evening, Penelope questioned her father while the family was having vegetarian franks and beans for dinner. "Daddy, I received information that my brother might be on the moon. A male by the name of Sam fits his description. Can I visit him if he is there?"

"Brother? I thought all Altwainians were female. Tell me about the males."

"A small number of Altwainians are males. After my Primterrean mother birthed me, she started to birth males. If you didn't already know, only Primterreans held in the highest esteem are involved in the birthing process, and males are birthed by the best of those. Sam was the first male my mother birthed, and we were very close during our educational period on Primterrea. We were even in many of the same classes, but unfortunately, we were sent to different planets and lost contact with one another. In a general sense, early in the Primterreans' growth of civilizations in the Milky Way galaxy, there was about a three percent male Altwainian presence in order to supervise the safe performance of strenuous manual labor. At that time, millions of Earth PIM years ago, there were dozens of societies being developed. Currently, there are only a handful of planets assisted by the Primterreans, so there is a diminished physical need, and consequently, Altwainian males throughout the galaxy total less than one percent."

"Victoria, contact Jones to see if Sam is on the moon."

"Done. And it does appear to be Sam."

"Then arrange for Penelope's transport for a personal visit."

"Done."

"And don't forget the flight requirements."

"Done. Daddy, you should know by now that we always comply with the regulations of both the Federal Aviation Administration and the National Aeronautics and Space Administration by filing flight plans."

"Thank you, Victoria."

President Carson realized the girls had set him up again—just like when Taylor was first introduced to him. Nevertheless, he still loved all his children.

When Penelope returned from the moon, Sam was with her. The president found it easy to tell Sam was a male since Altwainian males have an extra thumb on each hand. Dinner conversation centered on him and the moon work carried out by the

Altwainian males, who were highly qualified to perform the base's construction due to their geological knowledge and construction expertise on celestial bodies. The girls complimented Sam on his muscular arms. The president looked at Sam's skinny arms and thought, *Either I need eyeglasses, or the girls are hitting on Sam.* Several more compliments directed at Sam convinced President Carson that the girls were, indeed, hitting on Sam.

The girls educated Sam that in the recent past, Taylor and Penelope had successfully established and expanded their garment-manufacturing business; it was competing in the global fashion markets. The Altwainians now planned to break into the footwear industry. This major step required substantial planning from the chief executive officers of the apparel business, his sister and her twin, Taylor. Sam was extremely pleased and looked forward to an update the next time he visited Earth.

As vegetarians, Altwainians regarded activities such as fishing undesirable, due to the killing and consumption of fish; however, they found the sport itself relaxing. Taylor made use of the pastime by sunbathing next to a swimming pool in which Penelope was floating on a large inflatable duck while they discussed the shoe/sock business. This was the twins' equivalent of corporate executives meeting on a golf course to discuss a business arrangement. For safety, both girls wore life jackets since Altwainians had a tendency to sink in water. Taylor had a fishing pole with a hard plastic float on the line's end; it contained no hook. She would cast the line in Penelope's direction, who would grab and hold on to the line as her twin leisurely reeled her across the pool. A push with her leg against the pool's wall would then slowly send Penelope to the pool's far side, and Taylor would start the process again. The twins alternated positions hourly on a rotational basis. Since neither of the girls was adept at casting the fishing line, each occasionally hit the other on the head.

Because the twins were so excited about the plan they had formulated, they were not very hungry that evening and only had a small salad; Taylor had broken the coconut cream pie habit.

The president questioned them at the dinner table, asking, "How'd you get those bumps on your heads?"

After her explanation, Penelope said, "We've made a plan to begin manufacturing sneakers in order to have funds to help Altwainians settle in after the transition from Cimmaclay to Earth. We plan to launch the first manufacturing center on the African continent to create employment and, in years to come, build a strong middle class there, which is necessary for the establishment and secure foundation of democracy. The Altwainians emigrating from Cimmaclay will continue the age-old practice of craft production, with training of humans to take over the manufacturing of craft vessels for travel and exploration within your solar system."

Impressed by their dedication and consideration of the three species involved, their father simply said, "You're good girls." Remembering the countermagnetium incident in which he had complimented Independence with similar words, he added, "Just like Independence."

The months passed, and the day of the event anticipated with international glee soon arrived.

The wedding venue was on the first floor of the White House residence in the large East Room, which has a ceiling over twenty feet high. The first floor is where formal receptions of state are held; hence, it is generally known as the "State Floor."

As part of the bridal party, Taylor and Penelope had the responsibility of caring for the bridal train. They followed Svetlana to the altar and, upon reaching it, walked to her and said in unison, "We love you, Mommy." Carson experienced an intense feeling of pressure on his back and knew what it represented. He turned and nodded to the other three girls, who approached him and joined their sisters to receive hugs from the bride and groom. After vows were exchanged, the reception took place in the Rose Garden—the girls had guaranteed ideal weather conditions for the entire day.

Svetlana and Harold chose an appropriate site for their honeymoon, Earth's moon. Both were impressed with the view of their native planet. Victoria and Matilda had chauffeured them, along with several male Altwainians who had attended the wedding. The newlyweds enjoyed the four-week honeymoon but felt it went by too fast.

As the calendar pages flipped throughout the remaining portion of 2043, the Carsons announced the expected birth of a baby, due in May of the following year. Their daughter, whom they named Bridgette, was born on the Sunday before Memorial Day, 2044. A few weeks later, the couple celebrated their first anniversary with their six daughters—Bridgette and her five babysitters.

Eastern Europe was quickly becoming a vast global wealth center, with Midlandyya at its financial core. It would continue economic gains even without Svetlana, who chose to end her political career on a high note and raise a family; she did not run for reelection and would join her husband in retirement.

Senator Slick publicized his retirement rather than seeking reelection in the 2044 election; he had seen the handwriting on the wall when his crony, Senator Wiley, was defeated. One other notable retirement occurred simultaneously, that of Mr. Jones.

The girls were now developing an earthly sense of humor—they suggested throwing Slick and Jones a retirement party.

A SHORT STORY WITH SHORT ALIENS

PART V: THE POST-PRESIDENCY

After a successful second term in office, President Carson handed the reins of government to his successor. His wife, daughters, staff, and even Kitti, with play toy in mouth, had packed their belongings in preparation for their move from the White House; the Carsons relocated to their new home on Maine's coast. Although somewhat isolated, it provided the perfect environment for the girls to more freely use their interplanetary craft.

Former President Carson accepted a position as liaison to extraterrestrial civilizations. The following year, he was told a fleet of Primterrean mooncraft had temporarily entered the Milky Way galaxy as a stopover to a far galaxy. He informed the appropriate personnel of various bureaucracies to disseminate the information. Apparently, there was a flaw in the chain to distribute the news because when one mooncraft arrived and began to orbit Jupiter, astronomers were astonished at how an unknown moon suddenly appeared. At nearly two thousand miles in diameter, it rivaled Jupiter's moon, Europa, in size. A later investigation determined Senators Slick and Wiley had left a legacy of incompetent patrons who had not yet been weeded out of the government bureaucracy.

Sponsor extended an invitation to the Carson family to visit the mooncraft. She would transport them via her own mother ship. Victoria and Matilda navigated their craft and docked with Sponsor's vessel.

As the journey to Jupiter began, one particularly delightful incident occurred.

Sponsor welcomed them aboard, with special attention paid to Independence. It was the first time Carson had seen Sponsor in person, and he now knew she was a seven-footer, towering above everyone in his family. In the ship's low-gravity field, Sponsor was easily able to pick up, hug, and smother Independence in kisses. When she was put down, Independence was so intoxicated from her mother's love that she turned and walked into a wall.

Sponsor said, "Only Primterreans can walk through walls—like this."

Amazed, Independence felt the spot Sponsor passed through and received a tap on her shoulder. She turned and saw Sponsor pass through the opposite wall. Stunned, Independence stood in the room's center and did a 360-degree rotation, watching all the walls. She scratched the top of her head in disbelief when, suddenly, she felt the same spot scratched again. Looking upward, Independence saw Sponsor's arm retreat back into the ceiling. Still glancing upward at the latest area of attack, Independence started to giggle. She bent over and saw Sponsor tickling her ankles.

Harold said to Svetlana, "I never knew Independence was ticklish on her ankles."

Independence grabbed Sponsor's hand, pulled her up through the floor, and was once again smothered in hugs and kisses, to the enjoyment of Bridgette and her four other adopted sisters.

Svetlana said, "It looks like the Primterrean version of peekaboo that parents play with their infants."

Svetlana and Harold had played that game on many occasions with Bridgette, and as a baby, she loved it. Sponsor communicated to them that she was returning the delight she and Independence experienced when President Carson said to Independence, "You're the good one." That simple sentence meant the world to them.

Carson said to Sponsor, "I thought the Primterreans did not have intergalactic travel capabilities."

"We don't. Our home galaxy populates close to the center of other galaxies by use of a fleet of intergalactic vessels, each the size of a small moon, to transport all material necessary to start a new civilization. Due to the extreme difficulties in the construction of intergalactic vessels, none remain in the newly populated galaxy; they return 'home' to repeat the process in another galaxy. It took them ages to travel to this galaxy. The only reason that this galaxy received a visit for a second time is to transport a large group of Altwainians to another galaxy."

"How many mooncraft are there in your fleet?" asked Svetlana.

"Fifty," answered Sponsor. "It is the first time we have had so many. Five are new, and this is their first usage. They were built to replace the five aged original mooncraft slated for retirement. Only forty-nine will continue since one original mooncraft needs repair and will remain in this galaxy until capable of safe travel."

"Why are you gathering Altwainians to transport to another galaxy?" asked Svetlana.

"It seems that this galaxy, which humans call the Milky Way galaxy, is one of very few galaxies in which the inhabitants naturally have an internal life force like in our home galaxy. You refer to this as a soul. In most galaxies, that life force must develop on its own as an individual matures. We know that a single omnipotent force is responsible for the good spirit within beings—that is far beyond our abilities—but we do assist growth. It took Primterreans by surprise when we first started birthing Altwainians in this galaxy, and we communicated it to our home galaxy. The result is the second visitation to the Milky Way galaxy planned eons ago and now realized."

President Carson said, "It sounds like the Twains slated for repopulation elsewhere will be the catalyst responsible for disseminating good spiritual entities to another galaxy."

"Yes." Sponsor explained that only twice in all the galaxies settled by the Primterreans had there been a comparable situation in which an omnipotent entity saturated a galaxy spiritually. Just as in the two earlier instances, the Primterreans held the firm belief that it was a message to them. They further held that the Altwainians had matured into truly wonderful beings capable of disseminating their own goodwill by advancing other cultures. In both former instances, the previous biological species that the Primterreans birthed were given their independence from other cultures, and the same would happen with the Altwainians. The Primterreans had birthed a fourth biological species to assist them and replace the Altwainians leaving the Milky Way galaxy—they were part of the mooncraft fleet.

Hours later in Earth time, Sponsor's mother ship entered the Primterrean mooncraft orbiting Jupiter. Those aboard saw dozens, then hundreds more mother ships prior to docking. Carson realized there must be tens of thousands of mother ships contained in the vessel—and this was only one mooncraft!

Upon exiting the mother ship, the Carson family and Sponsor were ushered closer to the mooncraft's center. Sponsor telepathically instructed Independence to nod and smile to any Primterrean who initiated that courtesy. Passing numerous mother-ship commanders who precipitated the civility just communicated, both Sponsor and her daughter returned the acknowledgment. Independence told her mother she believed that the mother-ship commanders who began the greeting did so because Sponsor was greater in the Primterrean hierarchy than they were. Sponsor said Independence's understanding was mainly correct, but she added, "They greeted *us*."

The Carsons and their host were brought to another part of the mooncraft, which contained a communication area connected to the other mooncraft. They were told the Primterreans viewed on the screens were the commanders of each mooncraft, a position with extreme responsibility; every one of the commanders initiated their society's courtesy, which was returned by Sponsor and Independence. Their last introduction was to the leader of the fleet of mooncraft, a position near the pinnacle of the Primterrean social pyramid. They were aboard her mooncraft. Sponsor and this individual lightly touched arms, a greeting Independence recognized as an acknowledgment of equals. She had never realized her mother was so high in the Primterrean order, yet there it was. The leader then touched Independence's arm—she received a nod from her mother and returned the touch.

Independence questioned, "Why, Mother?"

Sponsor explained: "Altwainians never had a revered and competent leadership until you; they always looked to Primterreans for guidance. You, my child, have replaced us in that capacity. Our two cultures have always enjoyed a symbiotic relationship, disseminating goodwill to other societies. Primterreans recognize your goodwill capabilities and, as a result, have expressed their admiration of you by initiating greetings."

President Carson recognized that the Primterreans held Independence in high esteem. He realized they also regarded his "good one" as an equal. He suddenly understood the reason and thought, *Good golly, she's human in their eyes! They consider Altwainians humans just like I do.* Independence exhibited the desirable traits of the best of people: her goodness, sense of justice, trustworthiness, and love and respect for others; great organizational skills necessary for her leadership; and more. Carson further understood that he had, for years, overlooked the obvious: because the Primterreans considered the Altwainians their children and not their biological created entities, they *always* considered them people. The Altwainians continuously did what the Primterreans considered highly important—that is, they spread goodwill.

Across the Milky Way galaxy, each Primterrean mooncraft gathered millions of Altwainians interested in traveling to another galaxy destined to become home to them. It was a home of their own; they would not have to be the guests of other societies. The time approached for the optimum journey to the next galaxy. Sponsor, Independence, and Kitti were part of that migration.

It was a solemn farewell with tears filling both Carson's and Independence's eyes;

Svetlana openly wept. They all knew they would never meet again, but Independence had to live her own life, separate from her adopted parents. Furthermore, Independence had complete faith in her sisters to continue assisting Altwainians from Cimmaclay settling on Earth. The girls, in turn, knew Independence would provide the best leadership for the third-generation Altwainians in their own galaxy.

Kitti brushed everyone's legs as a good-bye gesture. Bridgette's parting words summarized the feelings of her parents and sisters when she said, "I love you, Independence."

Aboard mooncraft four, the mooncraft that remained in the Milky Way galaxy for repair, was a Primterrean who had birthed thousands of fourth-generation Altwainians. Her name was Mommy, and her "children" replaced the third-generation Altwainians, of which Independence was a member, leaving for a home galaxy of their own.

Mommy kept one of her children on the mooncraft in need of an overhaul. This fourth-generation Altwainian was Lo.

Lo, like other Altwainians in her generation, looked similar to the Twains of the previous generation—albeit about a foot shorter. In fact, Lo measured around the one-yard mark. In the rush to develop a replacement generation, Primterreans in their home galaxy had sent substitute Twains that should have been better developed. Lo was one of these flawed individuals, and although extremely brilliant, she lacked sufficient good judgment. Remarkably unheard of until this point in time, Lo's intelligence exceeded that of most Primterreans, and that's why Mommy kept Lo aboard mooncraft four, to provide input for the craft's restoration to service. At least, that was the official reason. The reality of the situation was that Mommy wanted to keep an eye on Lo due to certain exploits Lo had been involved in since arriving in the Milky Way galaxy.

Lo's participation in the mooncraft's repair centered on increasing its speed, which would be necessary for it to catch up to the rest of the fleet. Lo far exceeded this expectation and created a system that enabled mooncraft four to arrive in the

Altwainians' new galaxy centuries before the fleet. Mother ships fanned throughout the galaxy's center, searching hundreds of star systems and thousands of planets for those suitable for safe Altwainian habitation.

When the fleet of Primterrean mooncraft reached a location near the center of the destination galaxy, thousands of Earth PIM years had passed. After exploring scores of worlds found by mooncraft four, the Altwainians chose an uninhabited planet best suited for them. It was the second one they had surveyed and, quite coincidentally, was part of a solar system with twin stars. They would continue to advance the primitive cultures contained in the new galaxy, initially under the guidance of the Primterreans, until they began the journey back to the Primterrean home galaxy in the mooncraft with Lo's updated system. There was one notable exception: Sponsor stayed. The Altwainians received all Primterrean "birthments" and were now responsible for the propagation of their own people. Independence limited her birthing process to one Altwainian child so that she had time to dedicate to her, with assistance from Grandma.

There was one caveat to Lo's improvement to the mooncraft's drive system. It seems that when the updated mooncraft four was initially tested, Lo did the test without informing anyone, due to her flaw in good judgment. She was the only life-form aboard the mooncraft prepared for the sudden increase in speed. Millions of Primterreans and Altwainians were jolted from their stationary position and thrown against the walls, leaving permanent indentations in the outer hull. A safety feature in the inner hull prevented injury—except to their pride. As a consequence, when the mooncraft fleet returned to its home galaxy and the original five old mooncrafts were pulled from service, mooncraft four was the only one not dismantled. Instead, it was given a place of honor orbiting the ancient Primterrean home planet so that following generations could proudly point to the indentations of their ancestors in the hull.

LO'S GALACTIC ADVENTURES

Hi, my name is Lo!

LO'S GALACTIC ADVENTURES

PART I: LO'S NAME

A common misconception is that Lo's name is an acronym for "little one" because she is just under three feet tall. In actuality, Lo's name represents the initials for Leprechaun O'Hara. You're undoubtedly wondering how a fourth-generation Altwainian came by such an unusual name. This mystery can best be understood by a journey back in time.

It was somewhere in the neighborhood of two million years ago that the Primterrean home galaxy, Erstun, received a message from their citizens who had recently settled in the Milky Way galaxy. You may be aware that our planet, Earth, is located on one of the spiral arms in the Milky Way, the Orion arm. Earth is positioned over twenty-five-thousand light-years from the Milky Way's center. Primterreans initially establish their home base in a safe location near a galaxy's center and work outward making contact with indigenous cultures. Due to Earth's distance from our galaxy's center, hundreds of other civilizations were advanced by the Primterreans prior to us.

Aboard a mooncraft from Erstun was a Primterrean who had birthed thousands of fourth-generation Altwainians. They were slated to replace the third-generation Altwainians desiring to leave the Milky Way for a home of their own. Her name was Mommy, and she had birthed Lo, who, at that time, was nameless. Instead of providing a name when she met someone, Lo would say, "Hi, I'm a fourth-generation Altwainian." Mommy considered Lo her "baby."

During the journey from Erstun to the Milky Way, Lo had formulated a theory to immensely increase the mooncraft's speed. She discussed this concept with Mommy, who also thought it entirely feasible. Lo, realizing the importance of knowledge, learned every component of a multitude of subjects throughout the lengthy voyage.

Upon arrival of the mooncraft fleet into the Milky Way, each ship took a different path to inhabited planets containing Altwainians. Thousands of mother ships fanned out of each mooncraft and offered transportation to any Twain longing for a new home. On one world, Lo's wanderlust brought her to an area with multiple transient extraterrestrials. She saw a group of five aliens and introduced herself as usual. The leader said, "I never met a fourth-generation Altwainian. Are you as good as the third-generation Altwainians at repairing interplanetary crafts? Mine is sluggish at higher speeds."

Lo said, "I can not only repair your drive system, I can improve it!"

The alien was an Avaryte, the most greedy extraterrestrial society in the galaxy and the captain of the craft needing repair. He planned to have Lo repair the craft and then leave her on the planet without any compensation. Payment did not matter to Lo, she was happy to help. The Avaryte captain said, "Sure, if you can do both, that would be greatly appreciated. My craft is this way."

It took Lo but a few hours to repair and improve the interplanetary craft. She said, "Let's take it for a test."

As the interplanetary craft entered deeper into space, the captain said, "Looks like you repaired my craft. We'll return you to the area where we met."

"There's one more thing I have to do before we go back," Lo said.

"What's that?" asked the captain.

"I have to test the improvement to your drive system."

Lo implemented the updated functionality to the craft's drive system but failed to have the Avarytes brace themselves, causing them to impact against the craft's inner wall. Fortunately, the Primterreans designed all interior hulls with a safety impact feature to prevent injury if a being was thrown against it. The Avarytes left imprints of their bodies in the internal wall. Lo would repeat the same error in the future, and it would have historical significance.

Lo said, "It functions well!" She turned to look at the Avarytes' reaction and added, "Why are you hanging out against the wall?"

The captain sarcastically said, "It's our favorite pastime."

"Most unusual," said Lo.

As the captain and his four crewmembers took their positions, he asked, "Where are we? I'm totally unfamiliar with this star system—it's not the one we were in."

Lo said, "We just experienced interstellar travel. We are in a solar system with only one inhabited planet. It's called Earth."

"Impossible!" said the captain. "My craft is only capable of interplanetary travel—it does not have interstellar ability like a mother ship."

"It does now. That's the improvement I made."

"Incredible. Since we're at a viable planet, let's take a look and see how we can profit."

The Avaryte craft entered Earth's atmosphere and hovered above a Louisiana bayou. Lo and the captain were teleported down and walked through the marsh. Spotting a sleeping thirteen-foot alligator, Lo said, "Let's pet it."

"No, it may not be sleeping," the captain said. "Some animals pretend to be asleep as a ruse to capture prey."

He was right; the gator quickly gave chase to them.

"Up, up, teleport us up!" the captain yelled.

A ray of light targeted the two aliens as the gator opened its jaws in preparation to devour the captain. Suddenly, they were both on the craft, however, the gator was still about to enjoy a tasty morsel—the captain. The gator's head dropped, hit the craft's deck, and oozed its innards. Only part of the creature had been teleported, and it could no longer harm anyone.

The captain snapped, "Fourth-generation Altwainian, clean up this mess." He then commanded his crew, "Let's get away from this part of the planet and find a more civilized area."

The Avaryte craft headed north and then east, finally settling in upstate New York. As it lingered several hundred feet above the Catskill Mountains, Lo was teleported to the ground with the gator's carcass. Now that the reptile's remains were off the craft, Lo was about to request to be teleported back when she saw a small black-and-white striped animal. Lo took a few steps toward the creature desiring to pet the critter; it turned and sprayed in her direction—a few droplets wetted her. She immediately requested a teleport and was back on the craft.

The skunk's stench permeated the craft and the captain said, "This area stinks, let's go."

As the craft continued east over the Atlantic Ocean, its hypersonic speed soon brought it to the Irish coast. The Avaryte commander asked, "What is that stink? It smells worse in here."

One of the crewmembers said, "Our guest."

The captain turned and saw his indentation in the craft's wall, reminding him of a most annoying incident. He viewed an Irish lake in the distance, pointed it out to his crew, and said, "Give the fourth-generation Altwainian a bath."

With that command, Lo was teleported into a lake as the sun set.

An inebriated pedestrian saw the flash of light that teleported Lo into the water and went to investigate. He saw her floundering in the water. Lo, like all Altwainians, could not swim. She could barely keep her head above the waterline. Lo gasped for air, her life imperiled.

The drunkard walked into the lake until the water was at his knees, bent over, and said, "Here, let me help you stand."

With the assisted lift, the water came to just above Lo's waist. She took a whiff, and fortunately, the skunk's scent had dissipated.

The man said, "I'm Daniel. I'll take you to O'Hara's pub to dry off."

"Hi, I'm a fourth-generation Altwainian," Lo responded.

"We'll have none of that. I saw you ride a lightning bolt from the heavens and know that you were a man, reincarnated as a leprechaun. Don't make any mischief when we get to O'Hara's."

O'Hara's pub was being used as a funeral parlor with O'Hara's body present. At the bar were three men: Sean Sr., a seventy-eight-year-old farmer, his son, Sean Jr., and his grandson, Sean III. Sean IV, now at the ripe old double-digit age of ten, was expected to join them at the pub in a few years. Several other regulars were at tables.

Daniel introduced Lo to the bar patrons with the explanation of their meeting and O'Hara's reincarnation; they all accepted Daniel's words as fact. Then he explained bartending and O'Hara's business practices to Lo. He also showed her the backroom stock of liquor and a room filled with electronics—all the discarded gizmos from the village for the past several decades. O'Hara was a technology hoarder, and his pub was now Lo's new home and workplace.

Since the village had a population of less than one hundred people, O'Hara's was the only pub and designated as a male meeting establishment. Although the women of the village did not like O'Hara, who was a fifty-nine-year-old bachelor when he died, they all paid their respects.

What irked the village ladies the most about O'Hara was the words below his establishment's name on the window. It read:

O'HARA'S

THE SOBER IRISHMAN

EVERY IRISH WIFE'S FANTASY

The wives were particularly disturbed about the word "fantasy." They argued that if O'Hara had used the word "dream," they could have found that acceptable, although barely. The wives even lobbied O'Hara to change the wording—he would not budge.

The village ladies called O'Hara a "small man" because of his obstinacy. This was actually a double insult because of his height as well as his personality quirk.

When he was alive and asked his height, O'Hara would reply, "A hair over five feet." It was common knowledge that he was actually a hair over four feet ten inches. Because of his short height and mischievous personality, O'Hara was referred to as a leprechaun.

After O'Hara's funeral the next day, a small group of village men went into the pub and thought Lo was the strangest looking leprechaun they'd ever seen. Her looks were more acceptable the previous evening when they'd had their fill of good Irish whiskey and beer. A few hours and numerous drinks later, Lo's appearance was suitable again.

When the patrons placed an order, some called her "Leprechaun" while others referred to her as "O'Hara." A discussion started as to which name to call Lo, with Sean III offering a compromise. Hence, when Lo was mistaken as O'Hara reincarnated as a leprechaun, she was so named, using the initials for Leprechaun O'Hara.

Lo loved her new name, and from that moment forward, she would introduce herself by saying, "Hi, my name is Lo."

Sean Jr. said, "That calls for a celebration. Lo, pour yourself a double."

Lo downed a double shot of whiskey like a trooper, turned around, took one step, and fell flat on her face, unconscious. Daniel took advantage of the situation and yelled to everyone's delight, "Drinks are on the house."

LO'S GALACTIC ADVENTURES

PART II: LO'S FRIENDS

The bar patrons had wasted no time teaching Lo their drink preferences. They said that O'Hara was always generous in pouring a shot of whiskey even though he was a bit on the stingy side and needed watching when serving. Sean Sr. wanted to get every extra drop of beer possible and told Lo, "Make sure you always shave the head off every mug of beer you pour for me." They figured that with the shelves full of booze and multiple kegs of beer in the stockroom, Lo could afford to be lavish with the liquor, especially with Christmas in the near future.

Lo was accepted and made friends with the gents who were her regular customers. They shared pictures of their families with her, and she hung all photos given her above the bar. It made her happy each time she looked at one of the smiling faces. Lo began to like her new "home" but realized that she still needed to return to Mommy, as there was a lonely spot in her heart—Mommy was Lo's entire universe. Additionally, Lo knew that sooner or later someone would not believe the leprechaun scenario. Her plan was to use O'Hara's treasure of electronics to build a transport craft. Most individuals would have gone the simple route and built a communication device to contact others for help. Remember, Lo was a genius, but she lacked sufficient good judgment, and hence, the craft.

The vessel envisioned by Lo needed a large amount of a metal she realized was difficult to find on this planet—gold. Her first step was to invent a mechanism to find a significant amount of gold. With that done, she determined the largest cache was in the United States Treasury. Next, Lo developed another device to teleport the gold. She believed that because the United States had such a vast quantity, one or two bricks would never be missed. Accordingly, Lo "borrowed" some of the gold bullion needed to develop a mode of transportation from Earth to near the galaxy's center.

Weeks had passed since Lo first set foot on Earth and year's end was approaching; 2047 was on the immediate horizon. During the period she was missing, the Primterreans had scoured the solar system that Lo had visited, but to no avail. Multiple Primterrean mother ships had searched the system trying to locate Lo based on her unique brain waves—a method of extraterrestrial identification similar to fingerprints on humans. Their next step was to send thousands of fourth-generation Altwainians to planets seeking information on Lo. Finally, someone informed an Altwainian that Lo had gone off with the Avarytes.

Mommy was infuriated. She knew the Avarytes were the only society in the Milky Way galaxy that was openly hostile to the Altwainians. It was because of the Avarytes that the third-generation Altwainians developed the tenet to use only touch telepathy with other beings, unless the other party initiated telepathic communication. The reason the Avarytes physically abused the Twains was because the Altwainians telepathically determined the Avarytes were cheating other extraterrestrials in their commerce. The Twains informed the victims of their findings and trade ceased. When the Primterreans learned of the beatings endured by the Altwainians, they immediately evacuated all Altwainians from Avaryte locations for a period of one thousand Avaryte PIM years with the understanding that only a small number of Altwainians would return. Furthermore, other aliens refused to have any dealings with the Avarytes even centuries after the Primterrean quarantine period ended. The Avaryte economy nearly collapsed. As a result, the Avarytes obeyed any Primterrean request and immediately acted upon it.

Mommy stressed to her fellow Primterreans that, this time, they must deal harshly with the Avarytes. Apparently, the entire Avaryte society had not learned the appropriate conduct in relations with other civilizations. Both the Milky Way and Erstun Primterreans agreed to be sterner with the Avarytes.

Mommy's rage resulted in a demand rather than a request during a meeting with an Avaryte triumvirate. To drive her point, she communicated exclusively through telepathic means without regard to the Avaryte objections. Mommy had four other Primterreans aboard their mother ship supporting her, and they stood side by side encircling the three Avarytes. The sheer height of the seven- and eight-foot Primterreans was intimidating to the Avarytes—they were two to three feet shorter. Mommy demanded they find her baby; they agreed.

The entire Avaryte population was mobilized with the goal of finding Lo. Other extraterrestrials benefited from the finances the Avarytes were lavishly spending for information. Finally, the crew of a mother ship reported an unusual sight that proved fruitful. They had been engaged in trade near the area of the Avaryte craft Lo was seen entering, and they recounted a brief streak of light faster than any mother ship had whizzed by their craft. Backtracking the direction of the light, the Avarytes determined it originated from the area of Lo's last sighting. The flight's vector enabled the Avarytes to track the craft from one solar system to that of the sun.

The Avarytes reported their findings to the Primterreans. Mommy found the information credible because she knew Lo's theory to increase the mooncraft's speed was feasible. Furthermore, Lo had also stated to Mommy that she believed it possible to increase the speed of both interplanetary crafts and interstellar mother ships. Mommy's prospects of being reunited with her baby looked promising.

The Primterreans contacted Sponsor, their ambassador to Earth. She, in turn, contacted her daughter, Independence, who was adopted by former US president Harold Carson and his wife, Svetlana. Information was transmitted to Earth regarding Lo's brain waves and a match was found, in Ireland.

Lo's recovery was considered so urgent that Independence and her sisters, Victoria and Matilda, did not file a flight plan with either the Federal Aviation Administration or the National Aeronautics and Space Administration. Besides, Matilda was probably the best interplanetary craft pilot in the galaxy. The flight from the Carson's Maine coast home to Ireland was accomplished in minutes with Matilda putting the pedal to the metal.

Hovering over O'Hara's, the girls teleported Lo into their craft, at which point she said, "Hi, my name is Lo."

The girls introduced themselves and informed Lo of her mother's concern and the ensuing search. Lo assured the girls she was fine, she had made new friends, and she would share her experiences with Mommy when they were reunited. Lo wanted to do something nice for her acquaintances and did not want to leave yet. Independence agreed, but insisted that Lo speak with Mommy immediately since their craft had mother ship communication technology. The contact relieved Mommy's anxiety, and both looked forward to being together again. Upon termination of the communication, Lo asked, "What other updates are there to your interplanetary craft?"

Matilda briefed Lo on the craft's newest abilities, and Lo now knew what to do for her friends using the technology aboard the craft. Lo's solution also determined the fate of all the gold she had "borrowed" from the US Treasury.

A rumble and about three dozen jangles later, the village residents were awakened. It was too late for them to see the interplanetary craft fly off. Little Sean IV ran to the pub and found what was responsible for the jangles—pots of gold coins with each one containing a village lady's name. He pointed them out to his mother, who said, "Bless that sweet little leprechaun's heart."

Patricia, Daniel's wife, said, "And we thought our husbands' drunken ramblings about a leprechaun were just folklore nonsense!"

LO'S GALACTIC ADVENTURES

PART III: MOMMY'S WRATH

Independence and her sisters shuttled Lo to a mother craft sent to the Earth's solar system whereby Lo had another conversation with Mommy. Lo informed her mother that the updated Avaryte craft had an extremely powerful drive system. She indicated the craft exceeded the speed of mother ships and even approached the swiftness of a mooncraft on a "short" interstellar run. That's why the Avaryte craft was able to travel to Earth in just a few moments; the ship was now interstellar enabled. However, it was still not capable of intergalactic transportation.

Ordinarily, and if necessary, a mother ship could capture and hold a craft vessel. According to Lo, this was not possible with the modernized Avaryte craft, and the Primterreans needed two mother ships to seize it. Additionally, they had to capture it during a static moment, such as when it was orbiting a planet or moon. Mommy, with twenty mother ships at her disposal, ordered ten two-vessel groups to capture the rogue Avaryte. She was determined to see this scoundrel punished.

Once again, the Primterreans contacted the Avarytes and placed the burden on them to locate the renegade Avaryte. The Primterreans' principal focus was to have mother ships perform the actual apprehension and seizure of the craft with its innovative technology.

Both parties accomplished their missions just prior to Lo's return. Once reunited, Mommy and Lo's embrace lasted an unusually long period. Each had missed the other and were content if the moment never ended. Mommy had suffered intense agony while Lo was missing.

Lo became the chief witness in the Avaryte captain's trial. Testimony was also heard from multiple witnesses who provided information to the Altwainians, Avarytes, and Primterreans. Mommy testified and pointed an accusing finger directly at the defendant and said, "You abandoned my baby on a primitive world." The captain apologized repeatedly; he knew he was guilty and in the most serious of trouble. Never before had there been a Primterrean on the witness stand testifying against an Avaryte and one who demonstrated intense anger at him.

The Avaryte justice system found the captain guilty and recommended punishment. The captain would never command again, a penalty considered extremely severe in all extraterrestrial societies. Furthermore, they proposed subjecting the captain to detention on one of their sparsely populated moons—in effect, solitary confinement.

Lo's adoring personality intervened and asked to allow the captain to do something meaningful when she said, "Please, Mommy, don't have the captain isolated. He does have some good in him. Remember, he gave me the opportunity to prove *our* theory to renovate the interplanetary craft drive system, in order to increase its speed, was feasible."

The Avaryte justice system agreed to a modified punishment for the captain. Mommy, knowing that elderly third-generation Altwainians were in the process of relocating from Cimmaclay to Earth, insisted the captain do service helping them. After Sponsor and the relocated Altwainians agreed, he was transported to Earth. The expelled captain would spend the remainder of his days, supervised by younger third-generation Altwainians, aiding their seniors, who were "retired" from Cimmaclay.

Additionally, the Primterreans informed the Avarytes that they would retain the craft and its technology reengineered by Lo. The Primterreans would share it with other civilizations they deemed appropriate. They stressed that the Avarytes would eventually receive the updated craft knowledge *only if* their society exhibited benevolence worthy enough to earn it. To date the Avarytes had failed in that respect.

Like a thawing iceberg under the intensity of a strong summer sun, time melted months from 2047. The optimum point for the mooncraft fleet to travel was at hand. To flex their muscles at the Avarytes, the Primterreans did a flyby past the Avaryte solar system. Furthermore, the Primterreans informed the Avarytes that mooncraft four would remain on the outer rim of their system. The Primterreans wanted to ensure the compassionate development of the Avarytes by monitoring their society. It was also a good location to repair/update mooncraft four's drive system. Recommendations for improving the Avaryte culture would be left with the Milky Way Primterreans, who would ensure the proposals were implemented.

During every free moment, Mommy and Lo recounted their experiences while they were separated. One incident they both enjoyed was the fact that Lo left a few extra gold coins in Patricia's pot because her husband, Daniel, had saved Lo from drowning. Lo was impressed with her mother and all the time and effort she and the other Primterreans put into locating her baby.

Mommy said to Lo, "Of course I had to use all resources available to find you. Not only could you develop a significant improvement to our mooncraft drive system but because you're my baby, and I wish I was as brilliant as you."

Lo reached up and put her arms around Mommy's mid-thigh, snuggled up to her leg, looked upward, and said, "I wish I was as beautiful as you."

"Aw, baby."

LO'S GALACTIC ADVENTURES

PART IV: THE 3GA GALAXY

Although the Milky Way galaxy is enormous in comparison to many galaxies, the third-generation Altwainian (3GA) galaxy was far larger, even greater than the Andromeda galaxy, which is estimated to have twice the mass of the Milky Way.

As has been already established, there were two instances in which the Primterreans settled the first two generations of Altwainians in their own galaxies—their own home rather than guests of other societies. The same happened with the third-generation Altwainians, who desired to leave the Milky Way, when a fleet of Primterrean mooncraft made an unusual second stopover to the Milky Way and transported them to the 3GA galaxy.

After the Altwainians chose an uninhabited planet they thought best for their needs, which they named Altwainia, the mooncraft fleet began its unloading process. All cargo was a gift from the Primterreans, including approximately five hundred thousand mother ships. Each mother ship contained several interplanetary craft. About half of those vessels were converted to Lo's updated drive system during the transit from the Milky Way. Even under the watchful eyes of the Primterreans, it took experienced Altwainians craftspeople hours longer to convert each craft than it took Lo. The Twains were responsible for transforming the remaining interplanetary craft themselves, and that process would commence after settling in their new home.

The mooncraft fleet commander met with Sponsor and Independence to explain the procedure to establish the Altwainian's new home, which had PIM days and years very similar to Earth. She said, "It will take us about fifty of this planet's years to complete your home. This is about the amount of time it usually takes when we first create a society for our people in another galaxy. We expect to be here twice that period since we have to convert all mooncraft to Lo's new drive system. Independence, if there is anything the Altwainians need, let us know. As you are aware, once we commence our journey to Erstun, we shall not return here."

Housing was built, an agricultural community was established, and life's other necessities were created. Primterrean fine-tuned logistics made the Altwainian settlement process proceed smoothly and swiftly. After each Primterrean mooncraft emptied its bowels, it explored other galaxies in the immediate vicinity. These galaxies were mapped, and the best were identified for future Primterrean migration.

As the years progressed, the Altwainian birthing hospitals began to be used. Lo, interested in the process, spoke with Mommy about learning more of it. Mommy then contacted Sponsor and thanked her once again for her and Independence's assistance in rescuing her baby. Mommy learned that Independence was planning to birth a third-generation Altwainian in the coming days. Independence invited the duo to observe the process under her mother's supervision; Sponsor had birthed numerous Altwainians in her daughter's generation. Mommy, on the other hand, had birthed both third- and fourth-generation Altwainians and would note the differences to the other three participants.

Days later, the quartet met at the Altwainian birthing facility. Lo took particular interest in a tiny dot, smaller than a pin tip, Independence planted in her daughter. Lo asked, "What is its purpose?"

Mommy explained this was the reason Lo, and other Altwainians, promptly understood any spoken language—it was a translator. Lo subconsciously set her translator when dealing with other extraterrestrials, differing from Independence and her sisters. They had consciously set their translators prior to their contact with Earth and President Carson.

As Primterrean technology and scientific development grew, the translators and other functionalities had all been miniaturized further with the development of each Altwainian generation. Consequently, Lo's generation was a foot shorter than that of Independence.

Lo now understood why it was easy for her to communicate with nonpsychic extraterrestrials in their own language, but she still did not know why it was impossible to study the Earlies' language while on the voyage from Erstun to the Milky Way. A message from the Earlies was discovered just prior to the mooncraft fleet leaving Erstun. Primterreans believed the Earlies were a people who inhabited their galaxy before they evolved and were now in a different realm. Lo was interested in solving the Earlies mystery and would come back to this puzzle in the future.

In deciding a name for her newly birthed daughter, Independence thought of the precious time she had spent on Earth and, as a tribute to one value Earthlings held in high esteem, named her daughter Freedom.

Lo and Freedom immediately bonded and established a lifelong friendship. Lo also assisted in Freedom's education over the following decades.

One of their early scientific accomplishments was to clone Kitti, who was now an old-timer. Kitti's clone, or Kitti II, had all the same memories as her original. The two Kittis, while sharing Independence's lap, both requested a flannel pajama top to snuggle in. President Carson would have been driven mad had the two been in the White House at the same time.

One day, as Freedom's education progressed over the next few years, she asked

Sponsor, "Grandma, can Lo and I borrow one of your crafts to explore this solar system?"

Sponsor said, "Certainly, girls. Just make sure you're home in time for dinner."

Another of the friends' endeavors was that Freedom, with Lo's assistance, developed an interactive book that placed the reader in the midst of the storyline. The first book the girls used was one Lo had adored when she was on Earth. One of her newfound friends in O'Hara's had mistakenly left a present meant for his child in the pub. Lo found the book, read it overnight, and returned it to the owner the following day. It was the tale of two children about to be thrown into an oven by an evil witch. Freedom and Lo imagined themselves coming to the rescue of the children. Additionally, the girls, acting like mischievous children themselves, threw the witch into the oven. To them, the witch represented an Avaryte who had abused Altwainians; this was payback.

Lo and Freedom would never tell anyone of their secret fantasy, not even Mommy and Sponsor. It was theirs alone, and they chose to keep it to themselves. And besides, the Altwainians knew the Primterreans held their own secret.

LO'S GALACTIC ADVENTURES

PART V: THE PRIMTERREAN SECRET

The discussion of a Primterrean secret that many Primterreans were aware of, but few openly talked about, was the mechanism that further united Mommy and Sponsor. This incident happened after Independence birthed Freedom and the duo were discussing the process.

Sponsor said to Mommy, "Apparently, you are not aware that almost every Primterrean who births an Altwainian has at least one in which they deliberately bend the strict specifications established by the Birthing Council. The drawback to not adhering to those requirements is that in some way the newborn Altwainian is affected. I provided Independence with a bit more assertiveness than in the specifications. My belief was that she needed to demonstrate steadfastness with the Clayites. Although her ultimate success proved my thought correct, she suffered from depression when dealing with those on Cimmaclay who pushed back. I had many conversations with Independence to help her overcome her despair. On her own, my child would then always provide a solution to each obstruction presented by the Clays."

Mommy said, "In all honesty, I too did not follow the exact specifications when

I birthed Lo. I provided her with a much greater amount of intelligence than I should have, but I have not noticed any adverse effects on my baby. Please, Sponsor, be totally frank with me if there is something I don't understand."

Sponsor said, "Primterreans from both Erstun and the Milky Way are aware of your deviation of the Birthing Council provisions. No one in the universe is more intelligent than a Primterrean, and Lo's brilliance was an obvious breaking of protocols; however, our people appreciate the contributions that Lo has made to our society. Also, it is evident to Primterreans, and many have said it, that Lo lacks common sense. With regard to the specifications override you performed, our people have overlooked it since, after all, many have done the same as I already stated. It would be wrong if we chastised you, even though you have far exceeded the point any other birthing Primterrean has gone."

"I have never noticed that my baby has little common sense."

"You have been too involved with Lo and display an enormous amount of love to her. You need to take a step back to see her flaw," said Sponsor.

"I will try to take your advice, Sponsor, and I do appreciate your candor."

So began a lifelong friendship between Mommy and Sponsor that would extend over time and the massive distance of galactic space.

LO'S GALACTIC ADVENTURES

PART VI: THE ERSTUN GALAXY

With the passage of approximately a PIM century on Altwainia, and with updated drive systems to the mooncraft, the moment of departure from the 3GA galaxy arrived.

Farewells between Sponsor and Mommy were difficult and completely heartbreaking for Lo and Freedom.

The voyage from 3GA to Erstun took tens of thousands of years, a fraction of the time it would have taken without Lo's restructured systems.

The mooncraft fleet was celebrated upon arrival to Erstun by all the galaxy's inhabited planets, especially Primterrea Prime or, simply, Primterrea, the Primterrean's home world. The first planet within Erstun explored and settled by the Primterreans was called Primterrea One, the second was known as Primterrea Two, and so on.

Lo was renowned throughout Erstun for improvements to not just the mooncraft but also the interplanetary craft. The Primterrean governance looked forward to Lo's proposed update to the mother ship drive systems. They requested Lo work with a team of engineers, scientists, and technicians to accomplish this task. With hundreds of millions of mother ships converted and enabled to travel faster than the old mooncraft, fleets of mother ships could explore and settle numerous more galaxies in the universe than under the established method of mooncraft exploration, and in significantly less time. An additional benefit was that once the technology was disseminated to other civilizations, they would have access to intergalactic travel and they too would explore the universe.

Upon completion of the prototype mother ship, the day arrived for its test run. Mother ship technology capable of intergalactic travel was proved successful with Lo and a team of Primterrean scientists on board. They could not believe that the voyage to a neighboring galaxy was so smooth and swift—taking but a few moments and without any jarring movement.

Lo said, "Yes, we really traveled to a nearby galaxy. Let me prove it to you. I'll change the walls from opaque to clear so we can see our galaxy in the distance."

As the mother ship's wall became transparent, there was a sudden rush of escaping air. Lo quickly reversed the process and said, "That's the first time ever that I didn't take into account a conversion factor."

After the Primterrean scientific team got over their bewilderment from Lo's statement, they came to the realization that it was time to return to their galaxy.

The team leader said, "Lo, set course back to Erstun."

"Returning to Erstun was not part of the specifications you gave me," said Lo.

The scientific team failed to take into account one very important component of the experiment. It was also an omission on Lo's part.

"Well, can you return us to Erstun?" asked the team leader.

"If we had the material on board the mother ship, but we don't," she said.

"Navigator! Where exactly are we?" asked the commander.

"Good news. We're precisely where we planned—in the second-generation Altwainian's galaxy, which is near Erstun. They have a supply depot less than one Primterrea PIM day's journey by the mother ship's normal flank speed. Shall I set course, Commander?"

The commander, looking annoyed at being stranded in another galaxy said, "Yes, of course."

Prudently, the depot was contacted to ensure all necessary supplies and help were available. With assistance from the second-generation Altwainians, conversion for the return to Erstun was completed. The technology was slated to be shared with this galaxy first. They would use it in their exploratory mother ships to search out additional galaxies for civilizations to advance. This was the methodology established by the Primterreans eons ago and soon to be adopted by other advanced societies throughout the realm of Primterrean galaxies.

The mooncraft fleet's round trip from and back to Erstun took a considerable period. That epoch brought substantial advancement to the Erstun scientific community. It was believed that, rather than travel throughout the universe in spacecrafts, the entire Erstun galaxy could be used as a mode of transportation across the cosmos. Primterrean leadership believed it feasible; therefore, subsequent to the converted mother ship test flight, its proposition was disseminated throughout Erstun.

Lo and Mommy studied the proposal, and they thought there was a flaw in the Primterrean physicists' logic. They were invited to appear before the Primterrean Prime Elder Council, which had thousands of Primterreans represented on it from worlds within Erstun. Mommy, expecting the council to criticize and attempt to place culpability on Lo for the oversights related to the mother ship test flight, prepared to battle the council.

The council initiated their session with Lo and Mommy by complimenting Lo and thanking her for all her contributions to their society. It also approved Lo's recommendation for a safety net in case of an anomaly from the expected results, and, if she accepted, she was to be the chief administrator of the project. Mommy thought, *The council knew better than to criticize my baby and me.*

Lo chose the name *Project Antithesis* for her assignment. She also selected the Glees as the sole group to assist her.

The Glee civilization was located closer to the Milky Way's center than Earth. The average Glee stood about two inches shy of five feet; a height shorter than many other extraterrestrials and one others were comfortable with. The Glees had walnut-shaped eyes with crystal-clear irises, which enabled an individual to gaze into their virtuous depths and determine they were truly trustworthy. Similar to most telepathic species, their hairless heads were larger than human heads.

All other Milky Way inhabitants respected the Glees. Because the Glees always did their utmost to please other societies they dealt with, the other party returned the satisfaction. That is, with one notable exception, the Avarytes, who repeatedly took advantage of the Glees. This fact, along with the harsh treatment the Altwainians endured from the Avarytes, segregated the Avarytes from commerce with other aliens for centuries.

The Glees were interested in furthering their knowledge of the universe and had requested passage aboard a mooncraft. With a recommendation from the Milky Way Primterreans, a group of Glees were granted permission to travel to the 3GA galaxy followed by the journey to Erstun.

The test using Erstun as a mode of transportation required energy from all stars within the galaxy. As the experiment progressed, an unexpected result became uncontrollable. Instead of Erstun's movement, the size of the galaxy diminished. Lo, with the aid of the Glees, saved the Primterrean galaxy from further shrinkage and restored it to its original size using reverse-engineered energy from a black hole, which overwhelmed the energy from Erstun's stars.

A major aberration occurred as a side effect of the technique. Lo and Mommy were encased in a sphere that could not be penetrated by any method tried over the course of the next several days. Then days turned into months and years. It was apparent that the mother and daughter captives were surviving through the use of energy stored within the containment, as centuries became ages.

While in the sphere, Lo worked on many complex projects the Primterreans presented to her and Mommy. She even formulated a principle that the universe was circular and finite—not linear as was the theory at present. The overwhelming majority of scientists disagreed with Lo and continued their support of the linear hypothesis; only a minuscule group backed her new view.

The Primterreans found time travel to be one of the most difficult concepts to surmount. Although its premise was developed in the infancy of Primterrean civilization, they could never advance the idea to reality, that is, until Lo initiated its groundwork while in the globe.

The undertaking began with a communication center for interaction with past life forms. Once the desired results were achieved, the task to construct a teleportation portico began. Again, Lo's input led to a fruitful outcome. Unknown to Lo and Mommy, the Primterrean governance had a surreptitious motive behind its development; it was based on input from experts who had been working on the project to liberate the two captives from their containment orb. An obsession had developed with the Primterreans to free their hero, Lo. However, although considered an idol of the Primterreans, Lo always credited teamwork with Mommy and shared her success with her love.

Over time, Primterrean scientists suspected Mommy and Lo had unconsciously developed the containment sphere. They theorized that only an individual who both detainees had extreme trust in would have the influence to release them from that restraint.

Hence, they began the project to reach into the past in order to make contact with Sponsor.

The initial step for interaction with Sponsor was via the time communication device. The future communicators informed her of the situation with Lo and Mommy and explained their assessment of how it came about. They further told Sponsor of their belief in a solution for which she would be instrumental. Additionally, she could take her time in making a decision since it was irrelevant in time travel. The future Primterreans requested Freedom join Sponsor because Lo had always talked about how she'd assisted in raising and educating Freedom, and they had become best friends.

Upon next contact, Sponsor said she would travel to the future and Independence had given permission for Freedom to aid in the project. Freedom also wanted the opportunity to be with Lo again.

At the moment of the teleportation, a stowaway joined Sponsor and Freedom. When the threesome arrived in the future Erstun galaxy, Freedom bent over, picked up Kitti, and hugged her. She said, "I told you to stay home with mother!" Kitti's purrs spoke volumes that she preferred to be with Freedom—the feeling was mutual, and Freedom was happy that Kitti did not listen to her instructions.

With the successful transference of Sponsor and Freedom from the past 3GA galaxy to the future Erstun galaxy, they spoke with Lo and Mommy in the sphere.

Sponsor, in a private telepathic communication with Mommy, and Freedom, in a private communication with Lo, simultaneously said, "Read aloud the statement I'm about to show you."

In reaction, Mommy and Lo promptly said, "I'm out of the sphere."

Ding! That was the sound of the containment orb collapsing.

Freedom explained, "Since I was birthed, I had known of the extreme love you had for one another and your immense desire to be with each other in your own world. The excessive forces of the reverse-engineered black hole permitted the two of you to create that private world within the sphere. When each of you heard the other say you were released from the orb, you both instantaneously expunged your hold on the sphere so you could be outside its containment and with the other."

Sponsor and her granddaughter had promptly completed their mission—their return to the past seemed near.

Freedom was extremely happy to be in Lo's presence again, and Lo felt the same way. Freedom said, "I desire to stay with my old friend forever."

Sponsor knew Freedom was in good hands and would be safe. She inquired about her own return.

Lo said, "My theory to teleport an entity from the past to our current time was diligently developed by numerous generations of Primterrean physicists. It became more complicated with the distance from the 3GA galaxy to Erstun."

As each new team of scientists came to the containment orb for information during the course of their effort, Lo would use her standard introduction, "Hi, my name is Lo."

Lo added, "When the project was completed and checked, Mommy and I provided the final examination of all aspects to ensure it was successful. No one developed a methodology on reversing the process, but I can probably send you back in time to the point you left," said Lo.

"Probably?" questioned Sponsor.

Freedom telepathically said in a private conversation with her grandmother, "I have every confidence that Lo can return you to the past. Knowing Lo as I do from our interaction over the course of my early life, however, and her failure to take into account every detail of the spectrum involved, you may return as a microbe."

"I'll stay here with my granddaughter," Sponsor said.

Several meows from Kitti translated to "I'll stay with them."

There was something else that happened while Lo and Mommy were in the orb that nobody else knew about. During her life, Lo had repeatedly tried to solve the puzzle of the Earlies' language, but to no avail. She thought she had translated small portions of it, but these were incoherent, as if it were deliberately made so. While in the sphere, Lo got Mommy to participate in the translation venture immediately prior to Sponsor and Freedom's involvement to release them. This effort would soon prove fruitful.

LO'S GALACTIC ADVENTURES

PART VII: THE EARLIES

After their liberation from the sphere, Lo and Mommy completed their translation of the Earlies language but did not share its contents with anyone. Instead, they said it was their belief they could solve the mystery of the Earlies and travel to the area the Earlies occupied subsequent to the Erstun galaxy. Mommy had received a converted mother ship containing her baby's updated drive system—they would use it for transportation.

Sponsor and Freedom asked their two friends if it were possible to join them. Naturally, they received a positive response.

When it came time for Lo and Mommy to determine a conclusion to the Earlies' disappearance, Sponsor said, "Freedom and I discussed a premonition we shared. It was not egregious; on the contrary, we believe it was good. For that reason, we will not accompany you on the exploration seeking the Earlies."

"Lo and I appreciate all your friendship across time and space and are certain you are correct that the vision you and Freedom had in common was positive," said Mommy.

Sponsor's smile and wink gave Mommy the knowledge that Sponsor was probably aware that she and Lo were able to crack the Earlies' message and would not return. Sponsor's next words confirmed to Mommy that Sponsor knew everything when she said, "I know you will find happiness together for all time to come."

Sponsor's insight was only one of the many positive attributes that made her so endearing to Primterreans and known throughout the ages to many societies.

Months passed since Lo and Mommy departed the Primterrean home world. One evening, Sponsor and Freedom were stargazing. Freedom questioned, "Where do you think Lo and Mommy are?"

Sponsor pointed to the heavens and said, "Out there." She turned to a new direction, pointed, and said, "And there." Sponsor repeated the process again and again.

Freedom said, "You're right, grandma. They are everywhere and especially in our hearts."

When Lo and Mommy completed their travel, they found the entry point to a parallel universe, which they believed was the Earlies' home. Upon access, two figures appeared from an ultra-bright light; one was nearly eight feet in height, the other just under three feet tall. Lo took one step forward. Her short counterpart mirrored Lo's action, and they both said, "Hi, my name is Lo." All four individuals giggled. The other being stepped from her aura to reveal a second Mommy. They were future Lo and Mommy.

Future Mommy said, "It's good to meet you again."

Lo and Mommy returned the welcome.

Suddenly, two other figures appeared from the glow. The petite one said, "Hi, I'm a fourth-generation Altwainian."

Lo said, "It's good to meet you again, past Mommy and Lo. Come, let us view the past and future."

At a portal only steps from their meeting place, Mommy showed Lo her life's most precious occasion—Lo's birth. Mommy's two counterparts said the same.

Lo said, "And when I first opened my eyes and saw you, Mommy, it was love at first sight. My love for you has continued to grow since that point." Past and future Lo agreed.

The group continued to view past, present, and future incidents.

Future Mommy said, "Over here is when Lo and I developed the Earlies language. We deliberately wrote it as an inconsistent dialect so no others could translate our words. Not even my brilliant Lo by herself."

"It took the two of us to sit down and decipher the otherwise hodgepodge mixture of nonsense, each helping the other decode the portion we created," said present Mommy.

Past Mommy said, "Over here we placed the missive in the Erstun galaxy. It contained the instructions for passage to our universe. It was, and still is, a true enigma to all Primterreans."

Present Lo said, "I enjoy watching Mommy and myself deciphering that communiqué."

Future Lo said, "Mommy and I placed a suggestion in Sponsor's and Freedom's minds to not accompany us when we traveled in search of our new universe. It was no coincidence that they chose not to accompany us. That event is over here. Even more important was our contact with the Glees. We informed them of the proposed idea to move the Erstun galaxy and our concern of failure. The Glees were highly willing to prevent any harm to Erstun because they idealized Primterreans as well as all life. The Glees were instrumental in ensuring that the black hole's energy restored and saved the Erstun galaxy. An additional benefit to that vast burst of mega-energy was the creation of this universe; our place for happiness in a private setting."

At another gateway, past Lo said, "Look, Mommy, these are all my friends I made on Earth before aunts Independence, Victoria, and Matilda rescued me."

The group watched as Sean Sr. used his coat as a blanket to cover Lo, who was lying on the floor of O'Hara's—her reaction to the double shot of whiskey. Sean Jr., following his father's lead, put his coat under Lo's head, acting as a pillow. At the evening's end, they left Lo warm and comfortable and braved the cold night, coatless.

All three Mommys had the same thought: *What good friends Lo made.* They were happy Lo had left the ladies of the village each a pot of gold as a farewell gift.

Future Mommy asked the others to follow her and future Lo to a point they would find interesting. The mothers and offspring strolled quite a way, and time zoomed in the Primterrean universe—not in millennia, but in scores of eons.

Future Mommy said, "Here comes the Primterrean fleet of exploratory mother ships. It contains a large population of Glees, who eventually replaced the fourth-generation Altwainians. Those Altwainians, similar to other generations of Altwainians, chose their own galaxy to settle in and assist the less-developed inhabitants. Look there, there, there, and there. Those are the Altwainians' exploratory mother ship fleets converging with the Primterreans. Each group had been surveying the cosmos in different directions."

The joining of the multiple Altwainian civilizations with the Primterrean exploration group proved the universe was *not* linear in nature, but circular. How else could all these beings converge and at almost the same moment? They could not meet if it were linear. Therefore, the universe was circular and finite. The theory entitled "Lo's Hypothesis of a Circular Universe" was proven correct; her naysayers were wrong.

As the six strolled, they knew that, in their universe, time was meaningless. It was replaced by a power far greater: their love—maternal and offspring love.

They had created a world of their own in the sphere. Lo and Mommy, unknowingly, had also used the black hole's power to create their own private universe. They subconsciously knew the orb would eventually be breached and collectively desired a clandestine retreat. Their universe was that sanctuary. It was also the place they lived happily ever after: in past, present, and future time—in every time.

***

Thank you for reading *Short Stories: Including a Short Story with Short Aliens*. As this story demonstrates, a love between a mother and her child is universal and infinite. If you enjoyed it, you will probably like my next book, *A Soldier at War: The World War II Letters of Borys Bohun*. It is a love story, via correspondence, between a soldier and his fiancée, separated by more than three years of overseas duty. Its release is targeted for December 2024.

SCIENCE FICTION GLOSSARY

Altwainians: Also known as Twainians or Twains; beings who are birthed by Primterreans and have a strong desire to advance civilizations by aiding in the improvement of engineering, mathematics, sciences, and technological development of other planets. They do not harm any sentient being. Twains have telepathic abilities.

Avarytes: The greediest extraterrestrial society in the Milky Way galaxy and the only people openly hostile to the Altwainians. They do not have telepathic capabilities.

Birthing: Process that permits Primterreans to create or birth Altwainians in what humans would consider a hospital laboratory setting.

Clayites: Also known as Clays; residents of the planet Cimmaclay without telepathic skills. They look similar to humans but have bald heads that are slightly larger than humans.

Contact room: A communication center with interstellar capabilities and strict privacy. It permits lengthy conversations in a fraction of a second.

Countermagnetium: The key element necessary for interplanetary travel in craft vessels.

Craft vessels: Ships that are limited to interplanetary travel within a solar system.

Earlies: They were believed to be the original inhabitants of the Erstun galaxy.

Extraterrestrials: Intelligent beings from outside Earth.

Futorical: Documents that are historical in nature and based on events that will happen in the near future, soon to be the past.

Glees: An extraterrestrial telepathic species that always do their utmost to please other societies they deal with. They are trusted and respected by other Milky Way galaxy inhabitants.

Midlandyya: A nation in eastern Europe.

Mooncraft: The only vehicles capable of intergalactic travel; they are the size of a large moon like Jupiter's Europa—nearly two thousand miles in diameter. They can hold thousands of mother ships and numerous craft vessels.

Mother ships: Vessels used for interstellar travel; they usually have craft vessels contained within them for shuttle purposes to a planet's surface.

Planetary individual maturity (PIM): The aging that a person experiences on terrestrial bodies such as Earth.

Primterreans: The most advanced extraterrestrial civilization in the universe. The Primterreans assist other worlds with technological innovations. They have great telepathic capabilities.

***

PHOTO CREDITS

iStock photo 922779244, credit: Sarah5. Portrait of a gray alien standing and looking up at you.

iStock photo 867386102, credit: Sarah5. Portrait of an alien.

iStock photo 664532656, credit: Sarah5. Close-up portrait of an alien hushing with its finger on its lips.

iStock photo 504110140, credit: Orensila. Night sky. Stars in night sky.

ABOUT THE AUTHOR

James Bohun, a native of New York, graduated with highest honors from the City University of New York with a bachelor's degree in history. He began a career in government and worked in federal service for almost nine years, then worked for the City of New York for over twenty-seven years. Subsequent to retirement in 2015, at the age of sixty-five, Bohun moved from New York City to Tampa, Florida, where he researched, wrote, and completed this book. He can, therefore, be described as a successful mixture between New York's Big Apple and a Florida orange.

WWW.JAMESBOHUN.COM